Main Street

Staying Together

Also by Ann M. Martin

Belle Teal

A Corner of the Universe

A Dog's Life

Here Today

On Christmas Eve

P.S. Longer Letter Later
written with Paula Danziger

Snail Mail No More
written with Paula Danziger

Ten Kids, No Pets

The Baby-sitters Club series

Main Street #1: *Welcome to Camden Falls*

Main Street #2: *Needle and Thread*

Main Street #3: *'Tis the Season*

Main Street #4: *Best Friends*

Main Street #5: *The Secret Book Club*

Main Street #6: *September Surprises*

Main Street #7: *Keeping Secrets*

Main Street #8: *Special Delivery*

Main Street #9: *Coming Apart*

Main Street

Staying Together

Ann M. Martin

SCHOLASTIC INC.

NEW YORK ◇ TORONTO ◇ LONDON ◇ AUCKLAND
SYDNEY ◇ MEXICO CITY ◇ NEW DELHI ◇ HONG KONG

No part of this publication may be reproduced, stored in a retrieval system, or transmitted in any form or by any means, electronic, mechanical, photocopying, recording, or otherwise, without written permission of the publisher. For information regarding permission, write to Permissions Department, Scholastic Inc., 557 Broadway, New York, NY 10012.

ISBN 978-0-545-06897-0

Illustrations by Dan Andreason

12 11 10 9 8 7 6 5 4 3 2 1   11 12 13 14 15 16/0

Printed in the U.S.A.   23

First printing, April 2011

For David Levithan, for helping to bring Camden Falls to life.

Camden Falls

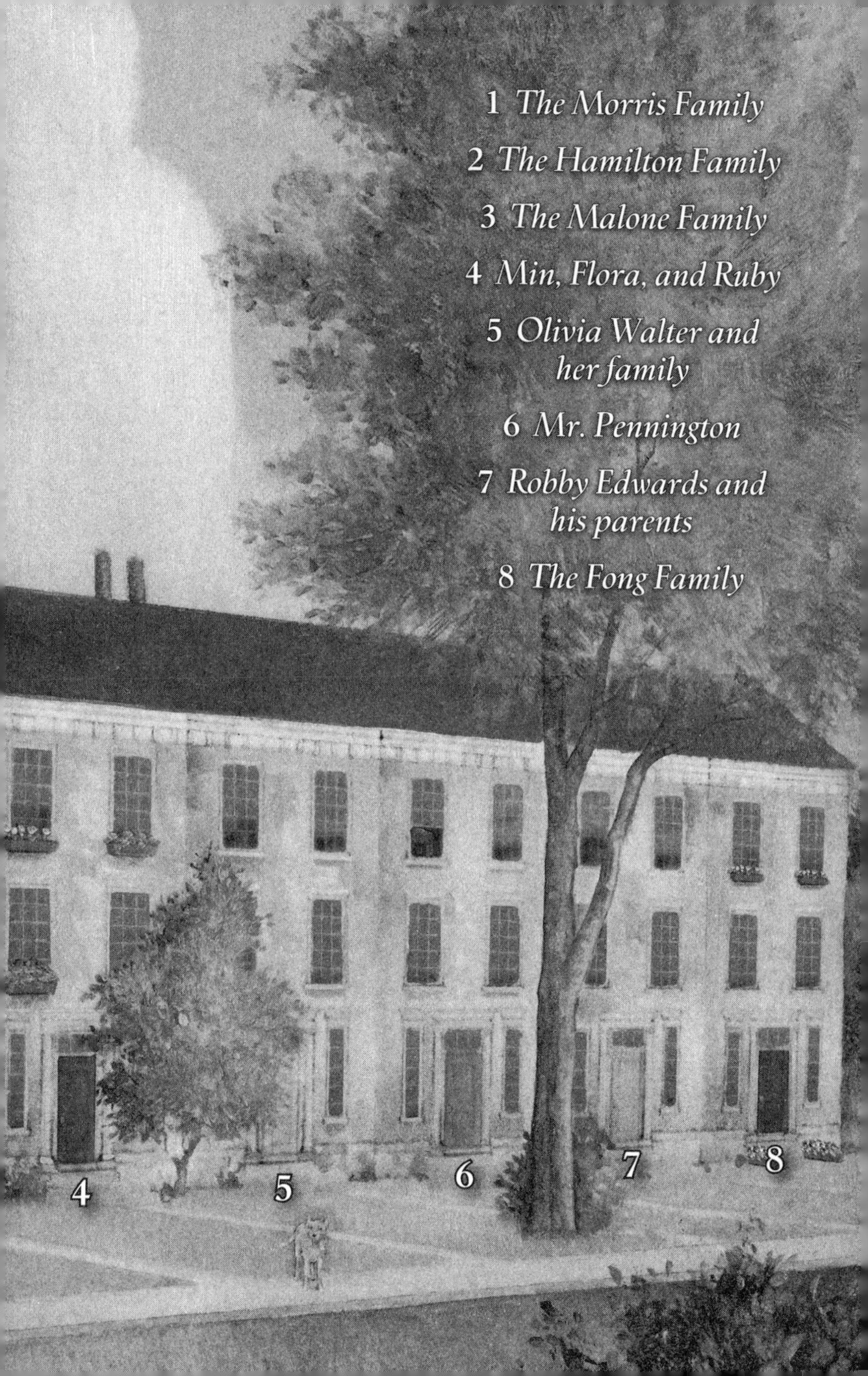

1 The Morris Family
2 The Hamilton Family
3 The Malone Family
4 Min, Flora, and Ruby
5 Olivia Walter and her family
6 Mr. Pennington
7 Robby Edwards and his parents
8 The Fong Family
4
5
6
7
8

CHAPTER I

A Peek in the Windows

Camden Falls, Massachusetts, is more than 350 years old, but some of the people who live in the small town think that only now is it starting to show its age. For three and a half centuries it has survived wars and fires and storms and floods, watched its residents weather heartache and sorrow, and rejoiced with them over births and graduations and marriages. During all those years, the town has stood sturdy and firm, even shone a little. But suddenly, now, cracks are showing in its foundation.

"It looks run-down," murmurs Min Read with astonishment as she rounds the corner of Dodds Lane one morning and turns onto Main Street.

"What?" asks Ruby, her granddaughter, who's walking into town with her. Min glances meaningfully at Ruby. "I mean, *pardon*?" Ruby corrects herself.

"Main Street looks a little run-down," says Min again.

1

"What does 'run-down' mean?"

"Shabby."

Ruby eyes the street. Camden Falls has been her home for only two years, but already she's proud of it. "It doesn't look shabby," she says, but even as the words are leaving her lips, she knows her grandmother is right.

In fact, much of Camden Falls is tinged with shabbiness these days. Times have been hard. As Min pauses on the corner of Main and Dodds, one hand resting on a lamppost, she notices things she's sure have been in front of her nose for some time but that haven't registered.

"Funny what you don't want to see," she says to Ruby as they continue on their way to Needle and Thread.

Ruby is silent for a few moments, not wanting to agree with her grandmother just yet. Finally, she says, "There are an awful lot of potholes in the street."

"Not enough money in the town budget to repair them."

"The paint on the lampposts is peeling."

Min nods. Quite a bit of Camden Falls could use a coat of paint. She sees that bricks have fallen off the fronts of several buildings, notes a broken pane of glass in the window of Time and Again, and sees a sign hanging lopsided from one hinge. Worse, two more businesses have closed since the holidays. And the Nelsons' diner, she knows, is in serious trouble.

"If we can hang on until summer," people are fond of saying.

No one bothers to finish that sentence, because if you live here, you don't need to hear the end. If the people of Camden Falls can last until the summer, then maybe the tourist season will pull them through. All they need is a slight shift in the economy — a slight positive shift, of course — and the tourists will flock to Camden Falls as they usually do. Then, perhaps, potholes will be filled and lampposts will be repainted and stores that are struggling will be able to come up for air.

Min Read is one of Camden Falls's old-timers. She has lived here all of her life, more than seventy years. Her store, Needle and Thread, which she runs with her friend Gigi, is holding its own so far, and Min knows they're lucky. The little deli on Boiceville Road closed after New Year's, and so far nothing has replaced it. The FOR SALE sign is still in the window, and the bay of the window is filled with mouse droppings. Around the corner from the deli, a gift shop has closed.

But come take a tour of Camden Falls and you'll see that despite its new air of shabbiness, the economy isn't the only thing on people's minds. Walk back to Main Street, turn onto Dodds, and retrace Min's and Ruby's steps to Aiken Avenue and the Row Houses, where Min and her granddaughters live in the fourth house from the left. Here are eight identical homes standing in a solid stone row. And in these homes live eight families — twenty-eight people — with very different things on their minds.

Peek in the windows of the house at the left end of the row and you'll find the Morris family. On this Saturday morning, all four of the Morris children are reading, even Alyssa, the youngest, for whom reading is a newly acquired skill. The Camden Falls library is sponsoring a kids' contest, and anyone who reads twenty books by the end of the month will earn a coupon for a free slice at College Pizza. The Morris children are determined to earn their slices.

Next door are the Hamiltons, the newest family in the Row Houses. They've been having a difficult time but not because of the economy. Mrs. Hamilton, who has been hospitalized after years of unstable behavior, will finally be coming home soon. Willow Hamilton, friend to Ruby's sister, Flora, isn't sure how she feels about this. She knows she *ought* to be excited — after all, her mother will finally be rejoining the family — but instead she fears that things will not be right after all.

Next to the Hamiltons are the Malones, and in this household there is a certain amount of excitement. Margaret Malone will be going to college in the fall, and she's preparing to leave the town she loves for a town that she hopes she'll love just as much.

Now, the next house belongs to Ruby and Flora Northrop and their grandmother Min Read. Ruby and

Flora are still considered newcomers to Camden Falls, having moved in with their grandmother after they lost their parents in a car accident. The last two years have been a time of adjustment for the sisters. Flora finds it ironic that just when she feels her life is settling down, she's having an awful lot of trouble getting along with Ruby.

Peek in the windows of the fifth house in the row and you'll find Olivia Walter. Olivia is a lifelong resident of Camden Falls — and Flora's best friend. She's noticed the trouble between the sisters, and she's determined to fix it. Somehow.

Next to Olivia's family lives Rudy Pennington. Rudy, the eldest member of the Row House community, is Min's dear friend. You'll find him sitting in an armchair in his living room. His favorite spot on a Saturday morning used to be the couch, but in the days since he lost his devoted dog, he finds that he can't bear to sit next to the empty spot that was once occupied by Jacques.

In the next house, the second from the right end, live Robby Edwards and his parents. Robby, who has Down syndrome, is excited because his mother has just shown him the flyer from Mountain View Center, where Robby has recently registered for the Special Olympics. "Look at all the activities!" says Robby. "They have a theatre class, too, Mom. And a dance is coming up! Can I go to the dance?"

In the very last house, Barbara Fong and her

husband watch their toddler, Grace, as she plods through the living room in search of a toy, then suddenly plops onto her bottom, well cushioned by diapers. "She's very tippy, isn't she?" says Barbara fondly. Her left hand is clasped in her husband's. Her right hand is massaging her belly.

On other streets in other houses, in town and in the countryside, life marches on for the residents of Camden Falls. In her isolated house bordering acres of farmland, Nikki Sherman — the fourth of the group of tightly knit friends that also includes Flora, Ruby, and Olivia — is contemplating her volunteer job at Sheltering Arms, the local animal shelter. She's remembering her promise to be on the lookout for a dog for Mr. Pennington, and she's determined not to disappoint him. Several miles away, in Three Oaks, the retirement community where Nikki's mother works, Mr. Willet — the former resident of the Hamiltons' Row House — slumps in his desk chair, eyes trained outside the window, and has the oddest feeling that something (but what?) is missing from his life. Back on Main Street, Hilary Nelson, eager to escape the tension that she always seems to feel in the diner these days, sees her friend Ruby on the sidewalk outside and rushes to meet her.

"Walk with us to Needle and Thread," says Ruby, and arms linked, Ruby, Hilary, and Min make their way along the street, trying not to notice the shabbiness that has crept up around them.

CHAPTER 2

Sisters

Flora Northrop, lying lazily on the couch in her living room on that same Saturday morning, reached for the telephone and dialed Nikki Sherman's number. She listened to the ringing of the phone, her hand absently patting the giant blond head of Daisy, Min's golden retriever.

"This is Mae!" a voice announced so loudly that Flora had to yank the phone away from her ear.

"Hi, Mae. This is Flora. Is Nikki there?" Flora crossed her fingers. If Nikki wasn't there, her sister, Mae, who was seven, was capable of talking at great length.

"Yes," replied Mae, and Flora uncrossed her fingers gratefully. "But do you know what?" Mae continued. "The Shaws invited me over and I get to spend the whole day at their farm. I can feed their chickens —"

"Mae?" (Flora heard Nikki's voice in the background.)

"— and groom their horse. I think I'll braid his mane. And usually for lunch we have —"

"Mae? Is that for me?" asked Nikki.

"— grilled cheese."

"Mae?"

"All *right!*" Mae exclaimed suddenly, and there was a fumbling and some rustling on the line before Nikki said, "Hello?"

"Hi, it's me," said Flora.

"Sorry about that. Mae's really excited about going to the Shaws'."

"If she's going to the Shaws', does that mean you're free today?" asked Flora.

"Yup. As soon as Mrs. Shaw picks her up."

"Is your mom already at work?"

"Yeah. Why?"

Flora groaned. "Oh. I was hoping she could drive you into town. Min and Gigi asked if you and Olivia and Ruby and I would decorate the window of Needle and Thread."

"I can come," said Nikki. "I'll ride my bike into town. The snow's all gone. Decorating the window will be fun."

"Excellent!" exclaimed Flora. "Come as soon as you can. The rest of us will be waiting for you."

Flora let Daisy out in the backyard, calling "Go pee!" after her. Then she checked to make sure the water bowl was full, patted King Comma the cat, who was curled up in a black-and-white ball underneath the kitchen table, let Daisy back inside, and ran next door to Olivia's.

"Ready?" she asked when Olivia answered the door.

Olivia was already shrugging into her coat. "Ready. Bye, Mom!" she called over her shoulder. She glanced at Flora. "Where's Ruby?"

"At the store. She went in with Min this morning."

Olivia paused slightly before saying, "Flora, are you and Ruby still —"

But Flora interrupted her. "What do you think we should choose as our theme for the window?"

"I thought Min and Gigi wanted something for spring."

"They do. But that's all they said. We could do so many things — butterflies, flowers, baby animals."

"Easter?" suggested Olivia.

"No, I think just generally spring. Hey, how about turning the window into a giant flower garden?"

"I like that idea. But doesn't the window also have to have something to do with sewing?"

"Oh, yeah," said Flora. "I forgot about that."

The girls reached the Morrises' house, the last in the row, and Flora glanced at it and recalled the first time she had ever seen the Row Houses. She had been a very little girl then, visiting Camden Falls with her parents and Ruby, who had been a baby. Flora had been fascinated, and slightly frightened, by the enormous granite structure, three stories tall. It had looked like a palace, far too big for one person, and Flora had been relieved to find that the old building in fact consisted of eight homes, and that Min occupied only one of them.

Flora had visited Camden Falls many more times before she and Ruby moved there after the accident. She was familiar with the Row Houses by then, and with Needle and Thread, one of her favorite places in the entire world. Flora loved to sew. How lucky, she thought, that she had wound up with a grandmother who loved to sew *and* who owned a sewing store. Min co-owned the store with Olivia's grandmother, but sewing was not an interest shared by scientific Olivia. Or by dramatic Ruby. Olivia would rather gather facts about unusual insects than thread a needle. And Ruby would rather sing and dance and act on a stage in front of a large auditorium full of people than look dreamily at bolts of fabric — something Flora could do happily for long periods of time.

"I have an idea," said Flora as she and Olivia turned onto Main Street. "We could stick big fabric flowers to the window —"

"How?" asked Olivia.

"I don't know. We'll figure that out later. But anyway, we'll use fabric — nice calicos in pastel colors — for the flowers, and then Min and Gigi and I can make spring outfits out of the same fabrics, and we'll display them behind the flowers."

"Oh, that's a good idea!" exclaimed Olivia. "But are you going to have time to do that and finish the quilts, too?"

Flora paused. "I guess so."

A couple of months earlier, when Flora had learned that Camden Falls's community center was in just as much trouble as some of the businesses that were closing, she had come up with the idea of making a quilt that would be auctioned off to raise funds for the center. One Saturday, the people of Camden Falls had dropped into Needle and Thread and created quilt squares showing scenes of the town and its history. By evening, enough squares had been completed to make two quilts, and Min and Gigi and Flora had promised to sew them together and finish them in time for an auction in June. It was a huge job — but Flora loved nothing better than a big sewing project.

Flora and Olivia reached Needle and Thread and stepped inside, shivering as they left the early April chill behind. The bell over the door rang, and Min and Gigi glanced up from the counter and smiled. Flora and Olivia waved to them. Then Flora's attention was drawn to Ruby, who was draped across one of the couches at the front of the store, listening to her iPod and singing under her breath, eyes half closed. Flora nudged her sister's ankle, and Ruby snapped her gum and opened her eyes the rest of the way. "What?" she said.

"Stop singing," Flora commanded. "People can hear you."

Ruby shrugged. "I'm rehearsing." Then she added, "But anyway, no one can hear me. I'm not singing loudly enough."

"Yes, you —"

The bell jangled then, and the Fongs entered the store, pushing Grace in her stroller.

"We just wanted to say hi," called Mrs. Fong. "We're on our way to the studio." The Fongs, who made furniture and jewelry, owned an art gallery and studio at the end of the block.

Min and Gigi stepped out from behind the counter while Flora, Olivia, and Ruby fussed over Grace.

"How's business?" Gigi asked Mr. Fong, which, Flora thought, was pretty much how all the adults in town greeted one another these days.

Mr. Fong looked thoughtful. "We're holding our own, I guess."

Mrs. Fong nodded. "Well . . . we're thinking of renting out the gallery space, though, and just keeping the studio. The gallery is expensive to maintain."

"But *you* don't have to worry about that, do you, Grace?" Ruby cooed. "Babies don't have to worry about anything."

Grace rewarded Ruby with a gap-toothed smile.

"All right," said Flora briskly, clapping her hands. "Let's get down to business." She plopped onto one of the couches.

"Down to what business?" asked Ruby.

"Decorating the window. That's why we're here."

"Well, excuse me if I don't understand every little thing you talk about," Ruby replied grouchily, and returned to her iPod.

"How are you going to help us if you're listening to music?" asked Flora.

Olivia stood up suddenly. "Oh, look! Nikki's here." She sounded relieved.

The Fongs left and Nikki entered the store, removing her hat, which caused her fine hair to dance around her face.

"Static electricity," said Nikki. "It's driving me crazy. I can't wait until the weather is warm again."

"Technically, spring is already here," Olivia pointed out.

"Which is why *we're* here," said Flora. "The spring window. Now, what I thought we could do is make a garden of gigantic fabric flowers, stick them to the window —"

"How?" interrupted Ruby, who was still listening to her music.

"Why does everyone keep asking that?" said Flora.

"It's a good question," said Nikki. "How are we going to stick something to the window? Anything we use — tape or whatever — is going to show through the glass."

"Huh," said Flora. "You're right. Well, we'll think of something."

"Maybe I don't want to make a garden," said Ruby. Flora glared at her. "Maybe the rest of us do."

Ruby shrugged again. "Okay. You guys go ahead."

"No, Ruby. You *have* to help us," said Olivia pleadingly. "Making flowers will be fun. Come on, let's go find the boxes of supplies in the storeroom."

Ruby got to her feet.

"Min?" called Flora. "Can we have —"

But she was interrupted by the jangling of the bell and turned to see Mr. Pennington.

"Good morning, girls," he said, removing his hat.

"Hi," replied Flora and Nikki in unison. Nikki added, "Nothing at Sheltering Arms yet."

"Well, I appreciate your looking — for an older dog," Mr. Pennington reminded her. "Since I'm older."

"I know," said Nikki. "No problem."

"And on the smaller side," added Mr. Pennington.

"I promise we'll find just the right one."

Mr. Pennington was still standing by the door when the bell jangled yet again and in walked Mrs. Grindle, who owned Stuff 'n' Nonsense across the street.

From behind her, Flora heard Ruby hiss, "Hide!" She turned to see her sister, who was struggling along an aisle of fabric with a carton labeled DECORATIONS, come to an abrupt halt at the sight of Mrs. Grindle. But there was nowhere to hide. Worse, Flora thought Mrs. Grindle had heard Ruby. Mrs. Grindle said nothing, though, just trained her beady eyes on Min and marched across the store.

"I have had it up to here!" she announced.

"Good morning, Gina" was Min's reply. (Flora stared hard at the floor. If she had looked at Nikki she would have started laughing.) "What's the matter?"

"Well, if it isn't one thing, it's another. People littering — *in the store*," said Mrs. Grindle. "People talking on their cell phones all day long, people looking forever and not buying a thing. What has happened to manners?"

"Yup. People are pigs," whispered Nikki, and Flora had to run to the storeroom so she could laugh without being heard by Mrs. Grindle.

The morning passed pleasantly. Mrs. Grindle finished complaining and left the store. Old Mary Woolsey stopped by to pick up a pile of clothing that customers had dropped off for mending and altering. Flora, Olivia, Nikki, and Ruby worked on the fabric flowers, and Flora and Ruby managed not to fight. At lunchtime, Olivia's father poked his head through the door. The Walters owned a store nearby called Sincerely Yours. Robby Edwards worked there part-time. "Hello!" called Mr. Walter, waving to Gigi, who was his mother, and tugging at Olivia's ponytail. "Stop by the store before you go home, okay?" he added, and Olivia nodded.

By late in the afternoon, the flowers were finished. Ruby had grown tired of the project and Min had given her permission to go to Hilary's apartment. Nikki hopped on her bicycle and headed for home, and Olivia left for Sincerely Yours. Flora had just sat down at the table in the back of the store and picked up several of the quilt squares when a shadow fell across her work. She turned around.

"Hey, Flora," said Margaret Malone.

"Hi," replied Flora.

"Boy, that's a big job."

"I know, but it's fun." Flora looked lovingly at her project. "Are you on your break?"

Margaret worked at Heaven, the jewelry store next door to Sincerely Yours.

"Yup. And I need stuff to make pillow shams. For my dorm room."

Flora looked at her curiously. "You got in?"

Margaret grinned. "I got in! In exactly five months I'll be on my way to Smith College."

"That's great!" Flora jumped up and gave Margaret a hug. "I know that's what you've been wanting, but . . . wow, I can't imagine going away from home. I wouldn't want to leave my friends and Min and everyone and go to a new place all by myself."

"You'll feel different when you're my age," Margaret told her. "Really. You'll be ready to leave. I'll miss my dad and my friends, of course. My sister . . . well, I guess that's a different story. Lydia and I have a lot of differences. I don't think we'll miss each other. But anyway, it's time for me to move on."

Flora thought about Margaret's words as she stitched away at the quilt squares. She and Ruby certainly had differences. They'd been drifting apart lately. Did this happen to all sisters? Flora hoped not. And she hoped that whatever had changed between her and Ruby could change back. But before that happened, Ruby had to fix the very bad thing that she had done.

CHAPTER 3

Keeping Secrets from Min

Ruby was in trouble. If only she could blame the trouble on someone else, but she couldn't. To her credit, she was trying hard to fix things. But if you listened to her sister, Flora, not only was Ruby *not* fixing things but she was a big, fat, untrustworthy liar. Which wasn't true. Well, not entirely. Ruby hadn't told Min a lie. She just hadn't told her something that, well, all right, Min would want to know about. But Ruby felt she could fix things without Min ever finding out what had happened.

This, however, was what always made Flora begin talking about sins of commission versus sins of omission — sins of commission being the bad things you actually do and sins of omission being the difficult things you *should* do, but conveniently don't. She made Ruby sound like a thieving, pillaging villain instead of a fifth-grader who had made a mistake.

As Ruby walked toward Main Street after school one Monday, she thought back to the afternoon when she had decided to entertain herself by looking through Min's drawers. She hadn't intended to do anything wrong; she had just wanted to see what her grandmother might be keeping hidden. Peeking in drawers was fun.

"Would you want someone going through your drawers?" Flora had asked her when she'd finally learned what had happened.

"I wasn't *going through* her drawers," Ruby had replied. "I was just looking."

"All right, would you want someone *looking* in your drawers? Me, for instance. How would you feel if you came into your bedroom and caught me pawing through the things in your desk?"

"Min didn't catch me, though," Ruby had said. "If you do something like that, you have to do it in secret. The trick is to avoid getting caught."

Flora had let out a sigh so enormous that Ruby had backed away from her because she could smell Flora's breath, and Flora had been chewing mint gum, apparently for quite some time, and it had a sour edge to it.

"Ruby, you are missing the point. Okay. Let me rephrase the question." (Ruby had decided not to ask Flora if she'd been watching courtroom stuff on TV again.) "How would you like it if you knew I'd been looking in your drawers?"

"But if I knew, that would mean I had caught you, wouldn't it? And I already —"

"Not necessarily," Flora had interrupted her. "What if I just *confessed* to you that I'd been going through — I mean, looking in — your drawers?"

Ruby had narrowed her eyes. "Have you?"

Flora had shrugged. And when Ruby had said nothing, Flora had smiled. "See? It doesn't feel very nice, does it?"

Ruby turned onto Main Street now and attempted to put the conversation out of her head. She was not a villain. All that had happened was that she had found a beautiful crystal owl in a box in Min's desk, had recognized it as something that had belonged to her mother (Min's daughter), and had borrowed it. Well, and then she had dropped it and it had broken into many pieces. Ruby had not panicked, though. She had thought about the situation in a calm manner and had decided to replace the owl before Min discovered it was missing.

"That is wrong on so many levels," Flora had said after Ruby told her what had happened.

According to Flora, what Ruby had done was wrong because:

A. She shouldn't have been looking in Min's drawers in the first place.

B. She should have told Min the truth right away.

C. The owl was in the box along with several other items belonging to Ruby and Flora's mother that Min had clearly been saving because they were special to her, and if Ruby replaced it with a different owl she was cheating Min out of something important.

But if Ruby managed to find another owl that looked almost exactly like the one she had broken, and Min never knew what had happened, what was the problem? Ruby was just trying to keep Min from getting upset.

Still, it was all very complicated, and on this afternoon, as Ruby headed into town to carry out her plan — to buy the replacement owl at long last and to sneak it back into the box in Min's desk — she wasn't entirely sure that what she was doing was right. Certainly, Flora thought it was far from right. But Ruby had worked awfully hard to earn money for a new owl — a new *and very expensive* owl. Which just went to show how much Min meant to Ruby. Ruby had been willing to work for weeks, months even, to raise enough money for a new owl. And in the process, she had tried to improve herself.

That was another thing Flora was conveniently overlooking. When Ruby had realized that she needed to correct her mistake, she had taken a good look at herself — at all her faults — and decided she needed improving. So she had drawn up a self-improvement plan, and it had been a huge success. She'd become neater, she'd brought her grades up, and she was working hard in her dance class and in the Children's Chorus at the community center. You'd think Flora would have been pleased that Ruby, who in November had been put on probation in the chorus after a disastrous performance, was now a regular member again and had even been given a solo in an upcoming performance. The performance was, in fact, to be a fund-raiser for the community center, the very same organization for which Flora had had the idea to make the quilts.

But no, all Flora saw was that Ruby had stolen (stolen!) Min's owl, broken it, was covering up her mistake, and was cheating Min.

Well, Ruby thought now, that was Flora's problem, not hers.

Ruby marched herself along Main Street. In her backpack was an envelope containing the money she would need to buy the owl she had found in Camden Falls's most expensive jewelry store and had put on hold several weeks earlier. The man who had waited on her in the store had been particularly unpleasant (Ruby had gotten the impression that he didn't like children), so Ruby felt she should get even more credit for having to deal with such an awful grown-up. That was how much she wanted to set things right with Min. She had braved *two* trips to the snooty store so far and had arranged for the crabby man to hold the owl for her, even when he clearly did not want to. She couldn't wait until she got home, secretly slipped the new owl into Min's box, and put the whole affair behind her.

Ruby walked by Needle and Thread, waved through the window to Min and Gigi, and continued along Main Street.

"Ruby!"

She had almost reached the jewelry store when she heard Hilary Nelson calling.

"Hi, Hilary." Ruby turned around and saw her friend hurrying after her.

"Where are you going?" asked Hilary.

Ruby paused. She had not told anyone except Flora about the owl, and considering how sorry she was that she had told her sister, she wasn't about to divulge the secret to somebody else, not even Hilary, who in the last year had become one of her good friends. Hilary's family had moved to Camden Falls from Boston the previous summer in order to open the Marquis Diner. The venture had not gotten off to a good start. Before the diner had even opened, it had been damaged in a fire. After it had been repaired, thanks partly to a lot of support from the community, it had opened and done reasonably well. But the economy (Ruby decided she hated that word) had not been kind to the Marquis.

"I'm just, um," (Ruby didn't want to tell an actual lie) "I'm just sort of taking a walk."

"Well, guess what," said Hilary in a dull voice.

"What?"

Hilary sighed deeply. "I didn't want to tell you this in school today because I didn't want to get upset. And just talking about it . . ." Hilary's voice trailed off.

"Oh, no. What? *Tell* me." Ruby pulled Hilary to a bench by a lamppost and they sat down.

Hilary sighed again. "Mom and Dad had a talk with Spencer and me last night." (Spencer was Hilary's younger brother.)

"Yeah?"

"And they said . . ." Hilary's voice wobbled. "They said . . ." Now she tugged at the zipper on her coat. "Okay, they said that they're going to see how the diner does this month. If we make a certain amount of money, then everything will be okay for a while. But if we don't make enough, then they're going to have to start thinking about moving back to Boston."

"You mean closing the diner?" yelped Ruby.

Hilary nodded miserably. "Not only that, but if we move to Boston, we won't be able to afford a house there until the diner sells, and that could be a long time. We sold our old house to buy the diner, you know, so . . ." Hilary shrugged.

"What would you do?" Ruby couldn't imagine being in such a precarious situation.

"Move in with my grandparents. I love them and everything, but they don't have a very big house — just two bedrooms. I don't know where we'd all sleep. And I don't want to start at *another* new school. Or leave Camden Falls. I like it here."

"Well, wait a minute," said Ruby. "Don't think so far ahead, okay? Your parents said they're going to see how the diner does this month, right? Maybe it will do really well. And maybe we can help it along. We could make special signs for the windows or come up with new sandwiches." Ruby desperately wanted to see a sandwich called The Ruby listed on the board above the counter.

"That's true," said Hilary, and she smiled. "Good idea!"

"Thank you," Ruby replied modestly.

Hilary ambled back to the Marquis then, and Ruby got ready to face the man in the jewelry store.

"Pretend you're about to go onstage," she said to herself. "Pretend you're getting ready for the performance of a lifetime."

She stood outside the jewelry store and took a series of deep breaths. In and out and in and out and in and out, she chanted slowly in her head. She closed her eyes briefly.

Just as she was starting to feel a calmness wash over her, the door to the store flew open and the horrible man stuck his head outside and said, "Excuse me, what are you doing, little girl?"

Ruby's eyes opened wide; then she glared at him. It was on the tip of her tongue to say, "Hello, I will be *e-lev-en* on my next birthday," but she remembered the owl and knew she had to do whatever was necessary to get it. "Sorry. Just enjoying the nice fresh air," she replied. "May I please come in? I'm here to pick up the owl. I have all the money."

The man said nothing but held the door open for Ruby, and she squeezed by him. Then she reached into her backpack and pulled out the envelope with the money inside. "This is what I owe you."

The man looked mystified. He stepped behind the counter, with its display of necklaces and rings and watches, and peered at Ruby over his glasses. "Excuse me?"

"The owl?" Ruby said again. "I put it on hold? I said I'd be in to pick it up in a few weeks? My name is Ruby Northrop?"

"Just a moment. Let me see if it's in the back."

See *if* it was in the back? It was definitely supposed to be in the back. Ruby felt panic rising. The man couldn't have sold it. He had said he would hold it for Ruby for a month. And the month wasn't even over yet. Not quite. Furthermore, it had taken Ruby forever to find an owl that resembled the one she had broken. She couldn't start the search all over again. Min might look in the box and discover that the old owl was missing —

"Ruby Northrop?" said the man. He was returning to the counter, and he was holding a box in one hand.

"Yes!" squeaked Ruby. "I mean, yes, that's me. Is that the owl?"

"It is."

Ruby sagged against the counter. Then she handed the man the envelope with the money inside. "It's all there," Ruby told him. "You can count it."

"Always a good idea," said the man, and he began counting.

Five minutes later, Ruby was walking out the door, a fancy shopping bag dangling from her wrist. She began to run down Main Street. She had done it. The owl was hers. All she had to do now was sneak it back into Min's desk, which wouldn't be a bit of trouble since Min would be working at Needle and Thread for another hour at least.

When Ruby let herself into the Row House, she was greeted noisily by Daisy Dear, who barked joyfully, and quietly by King Comma, who twined himself around her legs. "Hi, you guys," said Ruby. And then she called, "Flora?"

"In the kitchen," her sister replied.

"Okay. I'll just be in my room. I'm going to start my homework."

Ruby hung up her coat and flew upstairs. She closed the door to her room, tossed her backpack on her bed, and sat on the floor with the shopping bag. She drew the box out and opened it carefully. The owl was beautiful. It was perfect. It was not exactly like the one she had broken, but it was close, and she was sure Min wouldn't notice the difference.

Ruby set the owl on her bed, opened her door a crack, and listened for sounds from downstairs. Nothing. Cradling the owl in both hands, she tiptoed into Min's room. She knelt in front of the desk and silently slid the bottom drawer open. There was the cardboard shoe box with the fat rubber band holding the lid in place.

Ruby's heart was pounding and her hands had begun to shake. "Calm, calm, calm," she said to herself. She slid the rubber band toward one end of the box, praying that it wouldn't break. It didn't. She set it aside and lifted the lid. There were the other things belonging to her mother that Min had decided to keep: the snail shell, the bottle of perfume, the letter opener, the wooden box with a special penny in it. Ruby let her eyes wander over them. Then, very gently, she laid the owl in the box. She replaced the rubber band, slid the box in the drawer, and closed the drawer.

Done.

It was over. Ruby could end this awful chapter of her life and get on with things.

She stood up and turned around.

Flora was standing in the doorway.

CHAPTER 4

The Silent Treatment

Flora stared stonily at Ruby. "So you did it."

Ruby could feel herself blushing. "Well, I said I was going to."

"You really are something."

"Look, I'm just trying to keep Min from getting upset. Honestly, Flora, she isn't going to know that this is a different owl." Ruby paused. "You want to see it?"

"No, I don't want to see the owl! You just don't get it, do you, Ruby?"

"Get what?"

"What I've been trying to tell you all along. You are *cheating* Min."

"How am I cheating her if she doesn't even know what happened?"

"It's the principle of the thing."

"You know what, Flora? Shut up, okay? Just shut up. You talk to me like you're some kind of professor or lawyer, using words you know I don't understand. Do you like making me feel like a stupid little kid?"

"Do *you* like making Min feel — let me see, how can I say this so you'll understand? I was going to say *ignorant*, but instead I'll say *clueless*. Is that better? Do you like making Min feel like a clueless old lady, someone you can cheat? You do know what *cheat* means, don't you?"

"Yes, I know what *cheat* means."

"Well, I don't know if that's good or bad. My own little sister actually knows what *cheat* means and still thinks it's all right to cheat the person who's been taking care of her for the last two years. Min shifted her whole life around for us, Ruby. She was getting ready to retire. Her kids were all grown up, and then we came along and without one single complaint she picked up and kept on going. She put off retiring, she made a life for us here in her home —"

"Which is exactly why I don't want to upset her. You know, Flora, I think *you're* the selfish one. You talk about principles and everything, but if I tell Min the truth, she's just going to be sad. You want me to make her sad? Min's going to start thinking about Mom and the accident —"

"Don't you think she thinks about those things all the time anyway? *I* do. But maybe you've forgotten."

"Forgotten!" Ruby edged out of Min's room and down the hallway. Flora followed her. "Well, now you're just being stupid."

Flora stopped in her tracks. "*I'm* stupid. Huh. I'm. Stupid. The one who gets nearly straight A's. I'm stupid."

"There are different kinds of smart, Flora. Maybe you're smart in school, but right now you're being stupid about someone's feelings." Ruby paused. "And maybe I don't just mean Min's." She stomped into her bedroom and slammed her door shut.

Flora stomped into her own room and slammed her own door. Then she opened it, leaned into the hall, and yelled, "Don't think this is over." She slammed the door again.

Ruby opened her door, couldn't think of anything to say to that, finally shouted, "Snob!" and closed her door.

"Cheater!" cried Flora from within her room.

"Show-off!"

Flora didn't want to prove Ruby's point by coming up with a smart reply, so she flung herself on her bed and stared at the ceiling, fuming. After a while, she brought the phone into her room, closed her door again, and called Olivia. The moment Olivia answered, Flora said, "I am never speaking to Ruby again."

"Oh, no. Please don't say that," was Olivia's reply. "You don't really mean it, do you?"

Flora paused. "Well, it would be pretty hard *never* to speak to her again. I mean, we do live in the same house. But that's how mad I am."

"What happened?" asked Olivia.

"I can't say."

"Why not? We tell each other everything."

"This is . . . I'll tell you sometime. But not yet. I have to think about how to handle this. Ruby has really done it."

"Boy," said Olivia. "I hope you never get mad at me."

By the time Min came home from Needle and Thread, Flora had finished getting dinner ready, and Ruby, still sticking to her self-improvement plan, had set the table. These things had been done in complete silence, except for when Ruby opened the cupboard where the glasses were kept and accidentally bumped Flora's shoulder, and Flora had cried, "Quit touching me!"

"I thought you weren't speaking to me," said Ruby.

"And how would you know that unless you were eavesdropping on my phone conversation with Olivia?"

"You have a very loud voice," replied Ruby. (This was not true.)

"Well, anyway, stay away from me."

"You stay away from *me*."

"That would be my pleasure."

A few minutes later, when Flora heard Min at the front door, she said, "Do *not* let Min know we're fighting. She doesn't need that."

"I wouldn't dream of it," replied Ruby.

"That's just because you don't want her to find out about the owl. I, on the other hand, don't want to give her anything else to worry about it."

"On the *other* hand! What do you think I've been trying to do all this time? Anyway, I thought you weren't speaking to me."

"I'm not speaking to you starting right . . . now," said Flora as Min stepped into the kitchen.

"The table looks lovely, girls," said Min. "Thank you for making dinner."

"I set the table," announced Ruby.

"I made the pasta," added Flora.

"Well, it's all very professional."

Flora waited until everyone was seated and had been served and then she said, "Guess what."

Ruby looked suspiciously at her.

"What?" said Min, reaching for the salad dressing.

"I'm going to have my first true baby-sitting job for Janie."

"Really?" said Min, smiling at her granddaughter.

"Yup. On Thursday, Aunt Allie has an appointment with Dr. Malone. She says she'll only be gone for an hour or so and she asked me to baby-sit. I'll be completely in charge and I'll get paid."

"Gracious," said Min. "That's really something, honey." Min glanced at Ruby, who was staring stonily into her glass of water.

"Yup, a *real* sitting job," said Flora again.

"I started rehearsing my solo," Ruby spoke up. "You know, for the fund-raiser for the Children's Chorus. It's hard to believe that just a few weeks ago I was on probation, and now I have a solo. For the *fund-raiser*."

"Yes, lots of good news," agreed Min. "You two should be very proud of yourselves."

"Huh," said Flora, and Ruby took a swallow of water and started to cough.

By Thursday afternoon, Flora and Ruby had spoken to each other exactly twice. They'd spoken many times to Min in each other's presence, but their direct conversation had consisted of the following:

On Tuesday morning, Flora had tripped over Ruby's backpack, which was sitting in the middle of the upstairs hall. "Ruby!" she had yelled. "I nearly killed myself on that thing."

"Oh, darn," Ruby had replied. "Then it didn't work."

On Wednesday, Ruby had come running into the Row House and had collided with Flora in the front hall. It had been on the tip of Ruby's tongue to say, "Sorry." Instead, she said, "Can't you even stay out of my way?"

And Flora had replied, "That's a little hard to do when a buffalo comes through the door."

Then they had stuck their tongues out at each other, swiveled their heads around, and stomped off in different directions.

Now it was Thursday, the day of Flora's baby-sitting job, and she was determined that nothing would spoil this wonderful afternoon. For that reason, she was relieved that she wouldn't see Ruby after school. Ruby had a dance class, so Flora rode her bicycle peacefully to Aunt Allie's house. She noticed as she pedaled along that the first hint of green was appearing on the trees, that tulips were blooming in many yards, and that the buds on the azalea bushes were growing fat.

Fat buds made her think of fatheads, which of course made her think of Ruby, so she steered her mind in another direction. She thought about Willow Hamilton and wondered what would happen when Mrs. Hamilton came home at the end of the month. Flora knew Willow was nervous about the return of her mother, and she couldn't blame her. Mrs. Hamilton made Flora feel uneasy, and she wondered just how much Willow's mother could have changed in the past few months.

Flora turned a corner and spotted Allie's house. She saw her aunt sitting on the front stoop with Janie, who was bundled into her stroller.

"Hi!" called Flora as she coasted up the driveway and laid her bicycle on the lawn.

Her aunt got to her feet, smiling. "Are you ready for this? Ready to be in charge?"

"Absolutely. Don't worry one bit. Janie and I will be great. We're going to have lots of fun, aren't we, Janie?"

Flora peered at her cousin, who grinned at her from the stroller and said, "Ba!"

"Well . . ." said Aunt Allie, and Flora had a feeling that a very long good-bye scene might be coming up.

"Hey!" exclaimed Flora. "Aunt Allie, your appointment is in fifteen minutes. You'd better get going."

"Okay. You know where I'll be. And where the emergency numbers are. And where Min is."

"And of course I know that Mr. Barnes is right across the street," added Flora, glancing eagerly at the house of her English teacher. Her *single* and *very cute* English teacher, who would be the perfect husband for Allie and the perfect father for Janie.

Allie drove off then, and Flora sat on the stoop and faced her cousin. "It's just you and me," she told her. "Ready for a walk? Oh, look. There's Mr. Barnes now. Let's go say hi."

Flora thoroughly enjoyed her afternoon with Janie, not to mention the bills that Allie folded into her hand later. She was more than halfway back to the Row Houses before she realized that she hadn't thought about Ruby in almost two hours.

CHAPTER 5

Sarah

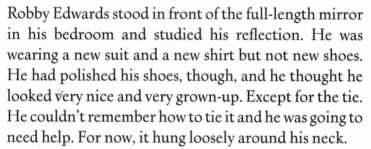

Robby Edwards stood in front of the full-length mirror in his bedroom and studied his reflection. He was wearing a new suit and a new shirt but not new shoes. He had polished his shoes, though, and he thought he looked very nice and very grown-up. Except for the tie. He couldn't remember how to tie it and he was going to need help. For now, it hung loosely around his neck.

"Okay," said Robby. "Okay."

He leaned toward the mirror and took another look at the tie. He had chosen the one with footballs and baseballs on it. Maybe that was the wrong kind of tie for a dance. Maybe girls didn't like boys who wore sports ties. And also, maybe his parents should have gotten him new shoes after all, but his father had said the old ones really were fine as long as Robby polished them.

Robby frowned. Then he opened his closet and looked at his tie rack. He saw the tie with the

Thanksgiving turkeys on it and the tie with the Christmas trees on it and the tie with the elephants on it and the tie that said HOME RUN all over it. And he saw the three ties that were just stripes. Robby pulled out the striped ties and ran downstairs with them.

"Mom! Mom!"

"Robby, goodness, what is it?" asked Mrs. Edwards, who was working at her computer in the den.

"Look at me! I can't tie my tie and I don't know which tie anyway and Dad said to polish my shoes but I don't want to wear black shoes. I want brown ones."

"Honey, calm down. First of all, you don't have brown shoes and we don't have time to go to the shoe store. We need to leave for the dance in twenty minutes. It starts at three o'clock. So the ones you're wearing will have to do. But you did a great job polishing them."

"Thanks," said Robby without smiling.

"All right. As for a tie, how about the one with blue stripes? They match the blue in your suit perfectly."

"Okay."

Robby stood still while his mother tied the tie. When she stood back, she announced, "Stunning!"

"Is that a good thing?" asked Robby.

"Absolutely. You look wonderful. Just think. Your first dance."

"Mom? What if there are no other kids with Down syndrome there?"

"Honey, the dance is at Mountain View. That's where the Special Olympics are going to be held. And that's where we've signed you up for volleyball. Mountain View is a place for all kinds of special kids, including kids with Down syndrome."

"What if I don't know anyone there?"

"But you will. I talked to Daniel's mom and he's going. And I'm pretty sure Rachel and Jason and Austin are going, too."

"Okay." Robby headed for the stairs. "I'll be right back. I need a few minutes of privacy time."

Robby closed the door to his room quietly and stood once more in front of the mirror. *A dance*, he thought as he looked at the shoes that were not brown and then at the striped tie. When Robby had been a student at Camden Falls Central High School, there had been lots of dances, but he hadn't gone to any of them. Most of the kids in school had been nice enough to him, but some had not been nice, and Robby hadn't wanted to risk seeing them at the dances. He hadn't wanted to hear their comments, either. Once, in the hallway, a boy he didn't know had said, "I bet you can't even put your own shoes on," which wasn't true, but Robby hadn't been sure what he should say back, so he had said nothing, and then the kid had slapped Robby's books out of his hands, and *then* he had said, "Why are you carrying all those around if you can't read them?" which wasn't a true thing, either, since Robby was the best reader in his class.

Robby was also exceptionally good at memorizing and had memorized a whole book of baseball facts, which was probably something the mean kid couldn't have done. But Robby wasn't sure how to say that, so he had just stood there until Margaret Malone had come along and picked up his books and smiled at him and walked him to his classroom.

Robby wished Margaret were going to the dance at Mountain View, but she was not. She was at work at her new after-school job, and in the fall she was going to college.

"Robby?" called his mother from downstairs.

Robby drew in a deep breath, let it out slowly, and said, "Coming!"

On the drive to Mountain View, which was exactly twenty-six minutes long, Robby's mother said to him, "I'll be right next door in the lounge, having coffee with Daniel's mother, if you need anything, okay?"

"Okay."

"Do you remember how to ask someone to dance with you?"

Robby nodded. "Yes. I say, 'Would you like to dance?' and if she says no, then I say, 'That's okay,' and I don't push things. But if she says yes, then I take her to the dance floor and we dance but we don't touch."

"You can put your arm around her waist," said his mother.

"No. That's okay."

Mrs. Edwards smiled. "All right. And when the music stops, what do you do?"

"I say, 'Thank you for the dance.'"

"Perfect. And maybe then you ask her if she'd like some refreshments."

"Okay." Robby closed his eyes. Then he opened them suddenly and exclaimed, "Mom, I've been waiting for this day my whole life!"

"Look, Robby!" said his mother as they pulled up in front of Mountain View.

A banner with the words SPRING FLING in pink and yellow and green letters had been strung over the front doors of the building.

"Excellent!" cried Robby.

His mother parked the car and they walked across the gravel lot to the wooden building that Robby always thought looked like a giant cabin. As they approached the front doors, Robby saw two girls wearing dresses that came down to their ankles, shawls draped across their shoulders.

"Very sparkly," Robby whispered to his mother. And then he added, "I think one of them has Down syndrome like me."

Robby and his mother followed the girls into the building. The lobby was crowded with young men in suits and young women in gowns and parents holding cups of coffee. Robby peeked into the room where the dance was to be held.

"Whoa, Mom," he said in a low voice. "You have to look in there. Just *look*, don't go in, because you're my mom and I don't want anyone to see."

Mountain View's largest room had been transformed. Enormous paper flowers decorated the walls and brilliant paper butterflies hung, fluttering, from the ceiling. A mirrored globe had been placed among the butterflies and pinpoints of light shot around the darkened room. Robby could see a refreshment table along one wall. A young girl handed him a glowing necklace. That was when Robby realized that there were glowing ice cubes in a bucket on the table and strings of bumblebee and flower lights everywhere. The entire room sparkled and shimmered and shone.

"Hi, Robby," said the girl who was handing out the necklaces, and Robby realized it was his friend Rachel.

"Rachel! I never saw you in a dress before," he said. "You look nice."

"And you look nice with just plain hair and no baseball cap."

"Thanks," replied Robby. He turned back to his mother.

"I'll be right over there," she told him, pointing in the direction of the lounge. "Have fun."

Robby stepped into the room alone. He glanced back once at Rachel, but she was busy handing glow necklaces to the two girls Robby had noticed earlier. Robby took another step forward. All around him kids were standing in groups, talking and eating. He didn't know any of them. Where was Daniel?

Robby heard music begin to play. Some of the kids started to dance. Robby looked toward the doors. His mother wasn't far away. Maybe he should find her and they should just go home.

"Excuse me, do you want to dance?"

"What?" said Robby.

A girl wearing a long yellow dress and silver sandals had put her hand on Robby's elbow. "Do you want to dance?"

"Um . . ."

"My name is Sarah."

"I'm Robby. I've never been to a dance before."

"Me, neither. Do you want to dance?"

"Okay."

This wasn't going the way Robby's parents had said it should go. Sarah had asked Robby to dance, not the other way around. But maybe it didn't matter. Sarah put one arm on Robby's shoulder and the other on his waist and he found that he didn't mind at all. He looked into her eyes, and she looked back at him, and they smiled at each other.

They began to dance. They danced four dances in a row and then they took a break for punch with glowing ice cubes in it. After that, they sat at a small table and Sarah said that she had graduated from high school the year before.

"Me, too!" said Robby. "From Camden Falls Central High School."

"I went to Kingston High. I have a job," added Sarah. "I work in the cafeteria. At my old school."

"I work at a store," said Robby.

He had about a million other questions to ask Sarah, such as what TV shows she liked to watch and whether her parents had said she could have an iPod, but Sarah said, "Let's dance again."

So they did. They danced and danced and had some more refreshments.

Robby could hardly believe it when the director of Mountain View stepped into the center of the room and announced that the dance was over. "Oh, no," said Robby. "We have to go."

"Will you call me?" asked Sarah. "I'll give you my phone number."

"Okay. I'll give you mine."

Later, when Robby was sitting in the car with his mother and they were pulling out of the parking lot, he fingered the slip of paper in his pocket and remembered Sarah's face as she'd said, "Bye, Robby. We'll talk soon, okay?"

Robby planned to call Sarah that very night. He would say "Thank you" and "I had fun" and "I hope we can see each other again soon." Maybe he would even buy Sarah a present the next time he was working at Sincerely Yours. He wondered what he should get for his very first girlfriend.

CHAPTER 6

Friends and Enemies

"What kind of changes?" Olivia asked as she and her parents and brothers sat around the dinner table one evening.

It was Friday night and lights were on in most of the Row Houses. Two doors away, Robby Edwards was whistling up the front walk with his mother, saying, "My first girlfriend, Mom!" At the other end of the row, the Morris kids were trying to convince their parents that they should go out for dinner. Couldn't they *please* go to the mall and eat at McDonald's? Next door, Flora, Ruby, and Min were in the kitchen. Min was stirring something on the stove, and Flora and Ruby had turned their backs on each other.

"Not big changes, honey," Olivia's mother replied.

"Is the store in trouble?" Olivia wanted to know. Please don't let Sincerely Yours be in trouble, she thought. It hasn't even been open for a year. We haven't given it a chance.

"It isn't in any immediate danger," Mr. Walter told her.

"The Nelsons might have to close the diner," Olivia's brother Jack spoke up. "Spencer said so."

"Well, we do not have to close Sincerely Yours," said Mrs. Walter.

"You said you have to make some changes, though," Olivia reminded her.

"That's true. We need to think very carefully about our overhead —"

"Oh," groaned Henry. "Not *overhead*. Don't use business words. I never understand what you're talking about when you use business words."

"All right. We need to be very careful about the money we have to spend in order to run the store. That's all. Tighten the store's belt a little," said Mr. Walter.

"How do you tighten its belt?" asked Olivia. "You're not going to fire anyone, are you?"

"No. We said we would make small changes, and that's what we mean."

Olivia believed her parents. But the thought that the store was in any kind of trouble at all disturbed her, and by Saturday morning she felt she needed some sort of fun distraction — something to take her mind off of inflation and recession and foreclosures and the economy and struggling people everywhere.

"A Saturday adventure! That's what we should have

today," Olivia said aloud, and the very thought of it made her hop out of bed and snap up the shade to see whether the morning was sunny. It was. Aiken Avenue sparkled in sunshine, and Olivia could see that across the street two of her neighbors were already working in their flower beds.

Excellent. Now — what kind of adventure should she and Nikki and Flora and Ruby plan?

Their Saturday adventures had begun the summer before when a nameless someone had arranged for the girls to be members of a secret book club. Every few weeks each girl received a copy of a book from an anonymous sender, and after they had read the book they were sent on a surprise adventure. Long after the book club had ended and the identity of the nameless someone had been revealed, the girls had continued the tradition of Saturday adventures, only now they arranged them on their own.

What could they do today? Olivia wondered. The adventure didn't have to be elaborate, and it would be a good thing if it weren't expensive, either. Just something fun. An afternoon at the movies? A trip to the mall, even if they didn't buy anything?

Olivia, still in her nightgown, brought the cordless phone into her room, closed her door softly, and punched in Nikki's number.

"Hi, Olivia!" cried Mae's voice. "I saw 'Walter' on the caller ID. That's how I knew it was you. Are you coming over today?" Before Olivia could answer, Mae continued, "You know what? I'm making macaroni jewelry. Would you like a necklace? Or a bracelet? I haven't figured out how to make earrings yet."

"Oh. Well, let's see. I would love a bracelet. That would be very nice."

"Great. Bracelets are two dollars each. You can give the money to Nikki the next time you see her."

"Um, okay."

"I'll get right to work on the bracelet. Bye!"

"Wait, Mae! Don't hang up. I need to talk to Nikki."

"Okay. Just a second."

When Nikki got on the phone, she said, "Did Mae make you order any of her jewelry?"

"Well, she offered to make me a bracelet and then she said it would cost two dollars."

Nikki laughed. "Don't worry, I'll talk to her. Don't you think she'll make a good salesperson someday, though?"

"I think she'll make a sneaky one. Listen, Nikki, I was thinking. Why don't we have a Saturday adventure today? We don't have much weekend homework and an adventure would be really fun. We haven't gone on one in a while."

"That's a great idea! What should we do?"

"I'm not sure. We'll all have to decide together. Maybe go to the movies? Or to the mall if we can find someone to drive us there? Or, I know! How about lunch at College Pizza? That wouldn't cost too much."

"I like that idea. And guess what. Mom isn't working today. She was about to go into town to run errands with Mae, so she can drop me at your house first."

"Perfect. While you're on your way over here, I'll call Flora and Ruby."

Olivia clicked off the phone, threw on some clothes, dashed to the kitchen, where she slurped up a bowl of cereal, and then returned to her bedroom with the phone. She dialed Flora's number and, as she often did, immediately put her ear to her bedroom wall and listened to the phone ringing next door.

"Hello?"

"Hi . . . Ruby?"

"Hi, Olivia."

"Guess what. Nikki is on her way over. We thought we should have a Saturday adventure today."

"The four of us?"

"Of course."

"As in you and Nikki and me and *Flora*?"

"Yeah."

"Nope."

"What do you mean, nope?"

"I mean I'm not going on any Saturday adventure if Flora is going, too."

"But that's what a Saturday adventure *is*. The four of us doing something fun together."

"Believe me," said Ruby, "if Flora goes along, then the adventure will not be fun for me."

Olivia let out a long, loud sigh. "We are not," she said firmly, "leaving Flora out of an adventure. We've never left any one of us out."

"Then I'm not going."

"Ruby!" exclaimed Olivia in frustration. Then she lowered her voice. "Put Flora on the phone, will you, please?"

Olivia heard Ruby set the phone down. Then she heard her call "Flora!" in an unnecessarily loud voice. And then, "FLORA!"

"WHAT?" answered Flora in an equally loud voice.

"PHONE!"

Olivia heard nothing more until, after a number of clicks, Flora said, "Hello?"

"Hi, it's me. What is going *on* over there?"

It was Flora's turn to sigh. "Just . . . nothing."

"It doesn't sound like nothing," replied Olivia. "But listen, I called because Nikki is on her way over and we thought it would be a good day for a Saturday adventure, but Ruby says she won't go if you go, and we're not leaving you out."

"Well, I won't go if Ruby goes."

"What? Are you kidding me?"

"No."

"You won't go if Ruby goes, and Ruby won't go if you go."

"Correct."

"But it isn't a proper adventure unless all four of us go."

"I'm sorry, Olivia. I don't know what to say."

"Olivia!" called her mother from downstairs. "Nikki's here!"

"Okay, thanks!" Olivia called back. She considered inviting Flora over, but she was feeling irritated with her friend, so instead she simply said, "Got to go. Bye." And hung up the phone.

"Nikki!" she exclaimed a few moments later when Nikki flopped into Olivia's armchair. "You won't believe this. Flora and Ruby are still mad at each other, and Ruby won't go on an adventure if Flora goes, and Flora won't go if Ruby goes. So the adventure is off."

Nikki's face fell. "What is wrong with them? What's the fight about anyway? Do you know?"

Olivia shook her head. "They won't tell me. But it must be bad. They're barely talking to each other."

"What are we going to do?"

Olivia picked at a bit of fluff on her bedspread. "I don't know. I guess we can only see Flora when Ruby isn't around and vice versa."

Nikki nodded dismally. "You have to admit that it isn't very pleasant when they're together."

"But I don't want things to change!"

"Oh, they'll get over it. How long do you think their fight can go on?"

"It's gone on pretty long already."

"Well, look. We don't have to let it wreck our day. Why don't you call Flora back and just ask her if she wants to go to the movies with us?"

"But we can't leave Ruby out of a Saturday adventure."

"Then we won't call it a Saturday adventure."

"Nikki. Ruby's not stupid. She'll know what we're doing. And she'll think we're choosing Flora over her."

Nikki, who had been sitting up straight, attempting to stretch her spine and therefore increase her height, slumped back in the chair. "I know. You're right."

"This is terrible."

"Yeah. Okay, then why don't we talk to Flora about it?"

"Because . . . do you really want to get involved with whatever's going on?"

"Well, no."

"Neither do I."

"So what are we going to do?"

"I guess you and I could go to the movies by ourselves."

"That's not what I meant!" exclaimed Nikki. "I meant, what are we going to do about you and me and Flora and Ruby?"

"I don't know."

"I don't know, either."

Olivia sighed. The day had been ruined.

CHAPTER 7

Top Secret

How was it, Nikki wondered, that a fight between two *other* people could make *her* feel so dreary? But she did feel dreary (Olivia did, too) and it was all because of Flora and Ruby. Everything was wrong. On Saturday, Nikki and Olivia had finally left Olivia's house and ventured into town, where they had each ordered a slice at College Pizza (not as a Saturday adventure but simply as a sad, second-place lunch). Flora had walked by on her way to Needle and Thread, seen them through the window, rushed inside, and slid into their booth.

"Why didn't you tell me you were coming here?" she had asked.

Flora had looked hurt in a way that instantly made Nikki feel cross, and she'd almost replied, "We don't have to tell you everything we do," but luckily had thought better of it.

Across the table, Olivia had shrugged her shoulders. "We didn't want to have a Saturday adventure and leave either you or Ruby out, so . . ." Her voice had trailed off.

"But this isn't a Saturday adventure."

"No. But you guys knew we were trying to plan one," Nikki had told Flora. "We thought if we asked you to come to lunch with us, then Ruby would feel hurt." She'd glanced at Olivia, who had said nothing further, and then at Flora, who had stared at the table. After a long embarrassing silence, Flora had said she'd promised to help Min with the quilts and had left College Pizza, looking tragic.

School the following week wasn't any better. Flora was glum, and the one time Nikki mentioned Ruby's name, Flora said, "So you're taking *her* side?"

"A, all I said was that the fight must be hard on Ruby," Nikki replied hotly, "and B, I don't know what the fight is about, so how could I possibly be taking *anybody's* side?"

Flora shrugged.

When school ended that day, Nikki couldn't wait to escape to Sheltering Arms. It was her afternoon to volunteer there, and she felt a wave of relief wash over her as the van from the shelter pulled up in front of Camden Falls Central and Harriet waved to her from the driver's seat.

Nikki waved back and slid in next to Harriet, who was practically a full-time volunteer at the shelter. "Thank you for picking me up," Nikki said. "Next week Mr. Pennington is going to drive me."

"No problem," Harriet replied. "It's been a busy day. I've been driving around all afternoon anyway."

"Making deliveries?" asked Nikki, and Harriet nodded.

Sheltering Arms supplied chow to people who could no longer afford to buy food for their cats and dogs. Nikki noted that the number of people who had applied for help had risen steadily in the past few months.

"Any new dogs come in this week?" Nikki wanted to know.

Harriet glanced at her. "You mean a dog that would be right for Mr. Pennington? No. Several new ones did come in, but four are large, two need a lot of rehabilitation, and the seventh is a mama with a litter of puppies. But don't worry. You know the perfect dog will come along eventually."

Nikki began each of her afternoons at Sheltering Arms in the same way. First she checked in with a young man named Bill, who was the volunteer coordinator, to find out what needed to be done.

"Just the usual today," Bill said with a smile.

"The usual" meant first checking the cages of the dogs that had been deemed adoptable, visiting with the dogs, cleaning up any messes, and refilling water bowls. After that, Nikki would enter the cat room, which was an enormous space inhabited by dozens of cats roaming freely in a feline-friendly environment. The room was full of climbing apparatuses, kitty condos, sleeping perches, blankets, beds, and toys. Again, Nikki would clean up messes, fill water bowls, and generally tidy things up. Often there were visitors in the cat room, people wanting to adopt, and Nikki and the other volunteers would talk with them and try to steer them toward the right cat for their family. When she left the cat room, she would set out for her favorite part of the afternoon — playing with the dogs outside in their runs.

Nikki and an adult volunteer left Bill and opened a door marked DOGS (which Flora once said looked like an entrance that was *for* dogs, not one that was *to* dogs). On the other side of the door were the cages for the friendly, adoptable dogs. Nikki had been pleased, the first time she'd toured Sheltering Arms, to find that the cages were more like small rooms. Some were even furnished with a couch or a chair. And each had a large, comfy dog bed, clean bowls, and a number of toys. Nikki started at one end of the room and worked her way up and down the row.

"Hi, Mystery," she said, reading the notice that had been posted on the door to the first cage.

Mystery, a large, very furry dog who looked like she might be part collie, greeted Nikki with a woof and planted her front feet on the ground, rump raised. She was ready to play.

"Okay," Nikki said, laughing, and started a game of tug-of-war with one of Mystery's rubber toys. Eventually, Mystery lost the game. She rolled over on her back and gazed soulfully at Nikki. "Belly rub?" asked Nikki, and obligingly patted Mystery's belly.

She moved on to the next cage, where she found a dog who looked like a mix of so many breeds that Nikki thought his name should be Mystery, too. However, when he had arrived at Sheltering Arms, he had been given the name Sparky.

"Hello, boy!" exclaimed Nikki.

Sparky tipped his tail at her, but he was in the middle of a nap, so Nikki patted him and left him alone.

Up and down the row she went, patting, talking, and playing with the dogs and chatting with other volunteers. Every dog was glad to see her, and by the time she walked back through the DOGS door, she realized that her dark mood had lifted.

She was working her way around the cat room again, rinsing off toys, sweeping up fur, and entertaining a pair of kittens who wanted to play with her dust broom, when Harriet entered, her arms loaded with bags of chow.

"What's the matter?" Nikki asked her. "Is something wrong?"

Harriet's face was grim. She set the bags down, then sat on the floor. Immediately, a cat climbed into her lap. She sighed, stroking the cat's back. "We just got a call."

Nikki could feel the bleakness return. She loved the shelter, but sometimes working there was sad, and the words *We just got a call* spoken in Harriet's dismal tone of voice never meant anything good.

"Dog or cat?" asked Nikki.

"Cat. Actually, a stray mama cat and three kittens."

"Are they sick?"

Harriet shook her head. "No. But a woman called to say that she's discovered the cats in her neighborhood and thinks someone is abusing the mother. The kittens are well hidden — smart mama — but when the mama goes out looking for food, someone keeps, well, torturing her. The cat is covered in scars and burn marks."

Nikki felt her stomach turn over, although it wasn't the first time she'd heard such a story. "So what's going to happen?" she asked.

"We're sending someone over to the woman's house right away to help her trap the mother cat. The woman knows where the babies are. The mother is wary, as you can imagine, but if we can lure her into one of the humane traps, then we'll bring her and the babies here right away. I don't imagine that will happen until tomorrow, though."

Nikki nodded. She felt like crying but didn't want to do that in front of Harriet. If you worked in a shelter you had to develop a thick skin. She brightened. "So the next time I come here we'll have more kittens!"

Harriet smiled at her. "Yes. And maybe you can help us work with the mother. It will take a long time to win her trust after what she's been through."

At the end of the afternoon, Harriet dropped Nikki off at her house. "See you next week," she called as she turned her car around.

Nikki gave her an over-the-shoulder wave and let Paw-Paw out into the yard. "You're lucky, boy," she told him. "You don't have to worry about where your next meal is coming from or whether you'll find a safe place to sleep."

Paw-Paw gave Nikki a doggie grin and followed her back into the house.

Nikki checked her watch. Her mother and Mae wouldn't be home for another half hour and they were bringing dinner with them, which meant that Nikki had time to start her homework. She sat at the kitchen table with her books stacked in front of her, stared at them for a while, and then picked up the phone.

"Olivia?" she said. "Hi, it's me. Listen, I've been thinking. We have to come up with a plan to end the fight between Flora and Ruby." She heard a muffled groan. "What, you don't want it to end?"

"Of course I want it to end," replied Olivia. "I just don't want to interfere. And I thought you didn't, either. You said so yourself."

"Yeah, but that was on Saturday. I thought maybe the fight would be over by now."

"I did, too. But look, if we get caught in the middle, that's just going to make things worse. They might get mad at us. Then they'd be mad at us, mad at each other . . ."

"Huh," said Nikki. "Maybe. But I think we can fix things without getting caught in the middle. For one thing, we *still* don't know what the fight is about, so it's impossible for us to take sides."

"I have a bad feeling about this," said Olivia.

"Well, just go along with me for a minute. What if . . . what if you and I plan another Saturday adventure, only we don't call it that. And then we invite Flora and Ruby — separately — to wherever our adventure is going to take place." Nikki paused, thinking.

"You mean so neither of them knows the other one has been invited?" asked Olivia.

"Exactly. And since they aren't talking to each other," Nikki continued, feeling inspired, "they won't find out that they've *both* been invited."

"I could call Flora and ask her to meet us at College Pizza," said Olivia slowly.

"And I'd call Ruby and invite her. I guess I'd have to tell her to come fifteen minutes later or something so that they wouldn't leave their house at the same time. That would make them suspicious."

"Yeah. . . ."

"But then eventually we would all be together and

we would have a great time and Flora and Ruby would see how silly their fight is."

"If it *is* over something silly."

"Yeah. . . ."

"What?" asked Olivia.

"Well, suddenly I don't know if this is such a good idea after all. You're right. They could both get mad at us for interfering."

"As I said."

"I know. I just want the fight to end."

"Me, too."

"This is starting to make me a little mad," Nikki admitted. "It's their fight, but it's affecting all of us."

"Yeah!" Now Olivia sounded angry.

"I have to go," said Nikki. "Mom and Mae just got home. I'll see you in school tomorrow."

Mae burst through the door then and exclaimed, "Mommy has good news, but she won't tell me what it is!"

Nikki tried to put Flora and Ruby out of her head. "What's your news, Mom?" she asked, smiling.

Mrs. Sherman set down her briefcase and a shopping bag from Bistro-to-Go. Mae tossed her school bag on the couch in the living room, turned three somersaults in a row, announced, "I want to take gymnastics," and threw her arms around her mother's waist. "*Please* tell us your news?"

"Over dinner," replied Mrs. Sherman.

When Nikki had cleared her books away and the table had been set rather sloppily by Mae and everyone had been served the fancy takeout food that Mrs. Sherman only bought on special occasions, Mae said, "Mom, please, please, please?"

Her mother smiled. "All right. Girls, you are looking at the new coordinator of dining services at Three Oaks."

"What?" said Mae.

"I'll oversee everything to do with dining and events."

"You mean now you're the Big Boss," Mae said with satisfaction.

Nikki leaped out of her chair and ran around the table to hug her mother. "You got a promotion!"

"A pretty nice one, too, I have to admit. It comes with a bigger paycheck, *and* I won't have to work on weekends so often."

"A bigger paycheck?" repeated Mae.

"Mom, that's great!" cried Nikki. "We have to call Tobias and tell him."

When dinner was over, Mae said she was going to make a special dessert and served up dishes of ice cream. She tried to spell out CONGRATULATIONS in chocolate chips on her mother's scoop, but only had room for the C, the O, and part of the N.

Nikki seized upon her mother's news as an opportunity to call Flora and Ruby. "I need to talk to both of you together!" she exclaimed when Flora answered the phone. "Something really exciting happened."

"Tell me, tell me!"

"Put Ruby on the phone, too."

There was a little silence. "I'm not speaking to her."

"You're right," said Nikki, already feeling exasperated. "*I* want to speak to her. I'm the one with the news."

But Flora refused to call Ruby to the phone.

"Okay. I'll tell you in school tomorrow," Nikki said abruptly, then hung up. She dialed Olivia instead.

CHAPTER 8

Welcome Home

One afternoon, when Willow Hamilton had been lying lazily on the floor of Flora's bedroom, Olivia, who'd been sitting at the desk, had asked, "How far back can you guys remember?"

"What?" Willow had replied.

But Flora had said, "You mean, what's our earliest memory?"

Olivia had nodded.

Flora had frowned. "Well, I can't remember anything from when I was, like, a baby. But I remember playing in the wading pool in the backyard at our old house one day. I think I was three. And Ruby had just learned to walk and she fell in the pool and my father screamed. It was the only time I ever heard him scream."

"What happened to Ruby?" Willow had asked.

"Nothing. My father had just panicked, even though he was only about four feet away. What's your earliest memory?" Flora had asked Olivia.

And while Olivia had told a story about getting her hand stuck in a jar of olives that her mother had specifically told her not to eat because they were for company, Willow had sat hunched on the floor, trying to invent an answer to the question. She certainly couldn't have told her friends her actual earliest memory. Even people who understood about her mother, which her friends didn't — not entirely — wouldn't have believed what Willow had to say. So when Olivia and Flora had looked expectantly at Willow, she had laughed and said, "My earliest memory is sitting on Santa's lap in a department store and telling him I wanted a credit card for Christmas. I didn't even understand what a credit card was, but I knew my parents bought all kinds of stuff with theirs, so I figured instead of asking for the stuff I'd just ask for the card."

Olivia and Flora had laughed, and Willow had not told them that the story was entirely made up and that her earliest memory was of hiding in her closet while her mother rampaged around Willow's room, yelling, "If you can't take care of your toys, then I'm going to give them to children who *can* take care of them." She had angrily stuffed things — Willow's teddy, her dolls, her princess wand, and other toys Willow didn't care to remember — into a garbage bag, which she took not to needy children but to the dump before Mr. Hamilton came home from work that evening. When her father had looked around her room and asked where everything was, her mother had said tersely, "We decided to have a cleaning-out."

● × ● × ●

Willow had grown up tiptoeing around her house — literally — unsure of what her mother might object to or what new rules she might suddenly put in place. Some of the rules made sense — like, take off your shoes before you come in the house. Others made no sense at all — inside doors must be left open at a ninety-degree angle, for example. Some rules stayed in place; others were eventually forgotten by Mrs. Hamilton, although not by Willow or Cole. Doors open or closed? Set the table with the dishes right side up or upside down? They never knew what might cause a burst of shouting or crying or a 5:00 a.m. phone call to neighbors.

Plenty of labels had been attached to Mrs. Hamilton's state of mind over the years as she had checked in and out of hospitals, but Willow hadn't paid much attention to the diagnoses. She'd just wanted to get through each day. She had enjoyed the calm, even days when her mother was gone, and she hadn't been sure what to think when her father had finally told her the exact date her mother would be returning from her most recent stay in the hospital, although she had been reassured by her father's insistence that things were going to be different from then on.

"I promise I'll be at home more," he had said, "and we're going to work much more closely with your mother's doctors." Willow had believed him. But as the day of her mother's return drew closer, she became more anxious.

And now today was the day.

"When you come home from school," Mr. Hamilton told Willow and Cole over breakfast that morning, "your mother will be back. I'll be picking her up in a couple of hours."

Willow glanced at her brother, who pointedly would not look back at her. "Want me to meet you on the corner after school?" she asked him. "We could walk the rest of the way home together."

"Okay."

When Willow turned off of Main Street that afternoon, she saw the small figure of Cole ahead. He was sitting on the curb on the corner of Dodds and Aiken, trailing a stick back and forth in the sand and dead leaves that had accumulated in the gutter over the winter.

"Hi!" Willow called when she spotted her brother.

He glanced up and waved at her but said nothing.

Willow was alone. Olivia and Flora had walked as far as Needle and Thread with her but then had gone into the store to visit their grandmothers. Willow was glad. She didn't feel like talking about her mother, and she certainly didn't want any worried glances when she and Cole stepped into their house to greet her after her long absence.

"Come on," she said to her brother, offering him her hand.

He stood up and brushed off his jeans but didn't take her hand.

"It's going to be all right," said Willow.

"How do you know?"

"Dad said things will be different."

"Maybe Dad will be different, but I bet Mom won't."

Willow began to feel annoyed. "Well, there's nothing we can do about it," she said. "She's home and that's that."

She marched ahead and had gone six paces when she felt Cole's hand slip into hers. They walked the rest of the way to their house in silence, but Willow smiled at her brother as they opened the front door. "Ready?" she said.

"I guess."

"Hello!" called Willow. "We're home!"

Cole closed the door behind them, and an instant later, Willow heard footsteps. Her parents hurried into the front hall.

"Oh," Mrs. Hamilton said, and put her hand to her mouth. "You've grown."

Willow could see tears in her mother's eyes. "Mom," she said, "you just saw us in March. We couldn't have grown since March."

"But you did!" Mrs. Hamilton pulled Willow and Cole to her and hugged them both.

"Welcome home," said Cole in a small voice.

Willow stepped back and took a good look at her mother, who seemed calmer than when Willow had last visited her in the hospital. And her attention was solidly on Willow and Cole. Not once did her eyes stray to the closet door, which was closed, or to the pair of sneakers Cole had left by the bottom of the staircase that morning.

"Come in the living room. Tell me everything," she said.

Willow glanced at her father, who smiled, and the Hamiltons sat down in their living room as self-consciously as if they were entertaining an unexpected visitor.

"Um," said Willow after a few moments, "I got an A on a math quiz."

"Good for you!" exclaimed her mother. "Bravo! We'll have to celebrate tonight."

"It was just a quiz, Mom."

"Nevertheless. And you, Cole. How is school?"

"Fine."

"Don't you have any details?"

"What?"

"Tell me about your friends, what you're studying."

Cole and Willow had spoken with their mother on the phone frequently in the past month, and she always asked about their friends and what they were studying.

"You know," said Cole, and Willow nudged him, but he shrugged and looked away.

"Cole has to give a book report on *James and the Giant Peach*," she told their mother. "And over the weekend he and Jack and Henry did something really cool. Tell her, Cole."

"We decided to have a drive at school. We're going to collect pet food for the dogs and cats at Sheltering Arms."

"You thought that up all by yourselves?" said Mrs. Hamilton. "Darling, that's wonderful!"

Cole dared to smile at his mother. And then he brought out his work folder from school and showed her his last month's compositions and drawings and book reports and quizzes.

At six o'clock, Willow's mother said, "What shall we have for dinner tonight? I'll cook."

"Oh, no," said Mr. Hamilton. "I'll fix something. This is your first night home."

"But I want to cook. I haven't cooked in ages."

"During the blizzard," spoke up Cole, "Dad let us make popcorn in the fireplace."

"In the fireplace?" exclaimed Mrs. Hamilton.

"We didn't have any power," Cole told her. "It was exciting."

"But in the *fire*place? That isn't —" Mrs. Hamilton stopped abruptly. "Well, I guess it doesn't matter."

"We were like pioneers in the olden days," said Cole, but Willow watched her brother's spirits fade.

She put a smile on her face. "Can I help you cook?" she asked her mother. "It would be fun."

"Of course," said Mrs. Hamilton, and the popcorn incident seemed to be forgotten.

Willow's family ate dinner together, and then it was time for homework and baths. Mrs. Hamilton seemed to be everywhere at once. She tidied up the kitchen with Mr. Hamilton. She sat with Willow, who was working on an essay and a math assignment.

"The rest of my homework is reading," Willow finally told her mother. Mrs. Hamilton didn't move, so Willow added, "I can read faster when I'm alone."

Her mother accompanied Cole to the bathroom. "Mom!" he cried. "I can take a bath by myself. I need my privacy."

"I'm just happy to be home."

Two hours later, Cole asleep in his room, Willow crawled under her covers. Her mother sat on the bed beside her.

"I'm so proud of you," said Mrs. Hamilton, and she smoothed Willow's hair back from her forehead. "Proud of you and Cole both. You've turned out just fine."

"Thanks, Mom."

Mrs. Hamilton kissed Willow's cheek, switched off her reading light, and moved quietly across the room. As she passed the closet she hesitated. Then she turned the knob, swung the door open, and left it at an exact ninety-degree angle to the wall.

"Good night, darling," she said.

Or Else

Flora's alarm went off shrilly and she lay in her bed, trying to keep her eyes open. If she closed them, she knew she would fall asleep again, even with the alarm blaring in her ear. She opened her eyes wide, actually held them apart with her fingers for a few moments, and then raised the window shade. Only then did she turn off the alarm. She sat on the edge of her bed before finally getting to her feet and stepping into the hall. The door to Ruby's room was open and she heard her sister say, "Rabbit, rabbit."

Flora frowned. "It isn't May first," she whispered loudly. "There's, like, eight more days of April."

Ruby rolled over in her bed. "I know. I just wanted to see if I could get you to talk to me. You really are terrible at the silent treatment."

Flora blushed and was glad Ruby couldn't see her face in the semidarkness. "Well, at least I'm not a liar."

"What? I couldn't hear you."

"I said, 'At least I'm not a liar.'"

"What?"

"I'm not a liar!"

"You're going to have to speak up," said Ruby.

Flora stomped off to the bathroom.

A few minutes later, on her way back to her room, she passed Ruby in the hallway and whipped her head around so that she was facing the wall.

Ruby whipped her head in the other direction.

"Liar," whispered Flora to the wall.

"I heard that."

At breakfast that morning, Flora sat next to Ruby instead of across from her. It was easier not to look at her that way. She speared her scrambled eggs ferociously, causing them to skid across her plate and onto the table.

Ruby giggled.

Flora scooped them into her napkin and emptied the napkin onto Ruby's plate.

"Flora!" exclaimed Min.

"Well, would you want someone to laugh at you if you made a mistake?"

Min looked thoughtful. "I might try to have a sense of humor about it. Flora, please get Ruby another plate and give her some more eggs."

"Thank you, Min. I appreciate that," Ruby replied meekly. She said nothing, however, when Flora set the clean plate in front of her.

"You're welcome," said Flora loudly.

Min eyed Flora over her reading glasses. "Anything wrong?"

"Nope."

"Ruby? Anything wrong at your end?"

"Nope."

"I highly doubt that."

"Actually," Flora replied, "there is a slight problem. I think there's something Ruby wants to tell you."

"No! No, there isn't!" yelped Ruby. "Everything's fine, Min. I promise. Sorry, Flora. Sorry for teasing you. I shouldn't have done that."

"Thank you for apologizing, Ruby. That's very nice of you," said Min.

"Um, I'm sorry, too," Flora said, managing a glance in Ruby's direction.

"You know, your mother and Aunt Allie used to fight," commented Min.

"Really?" said Flora with interest.

"Like cats and dogs."

Ruby glanced down at King Comma and Daisy, who were seated side by side, patiently waiting for someone to be clumsy enough to drop food onto the floor. Every now and then King would glance at Daisy or vice versa. It was as if they were holding a conversation with their eyes.

I thought those eggs were going to land on the floor.

Me, too. Bad luck. Remember that time a whole muffin fell down?

Like it was yesterday.

"King and Daisy don't fight," Ruby pointed out. "Not anymore, anyway."

"It's just an expression," replied Min. "The point is that your mother and Aunt Allie used to have big fights. Once they didn't speak for nearly two months."

"Why not?" asked Flora.

"Something about a boy."

Ruby rolled her eyes. "Boys," she said, "are not worth fighting about."

It was on the tip of Flora's tongue to say that lying *was* worth fighting about, but Min went on, "It's usually better to get things out in the open."

"Usually," echoed Flora, and now she looked pointedly at Ruby, but Ruby was suddenly very busy opening a jar of jam.

Flora took great pride in the fact that she had recently become a working girl. She volunteered at Three Oaks, where her old Row House neighbors, Mr. and Mrs. Willet, now lived. Once a week, Mr. Pennington drove Flora to the retirement community, and while Flora donned her Helping Hand apron and delivered flowers and pushed wheelchairs and re-shelved books in the library, Mr. Pennington visited with Mr. Willet.

"See you in two hours!" Flora called to Mr. Pennington one afternoon as he stepped into the elevator. She wound her way through the corridors to the front desk at Three Oaks and greeted Dee, who was typing at a computer. "Hi," Flora said. "What do you want me to do today?"

Dee smiled at her. "We're busy. And we're short-handed. Could you help set up chairs in the auditorium? We're having a speaker tonight."

"Sure," Flora replied. She spent the next half hour happily arranging rows of chairs in the auditorium. After that, she stapled together two hundred copies of Three Oaks's weekly bulletin; read to Mr. Cooke, who was ninety-nine years old, completely blind, and said he couldn't live without a daily dose of Shakespeare (Flora was pretty sure she had mispronounced quite a few words, but Mr. Cooke didn't complain); and finally decided to visit Mrs. Willet in her room in the wing for people with Alzheimer's disease.

Flora let herself into the wing by punching in a code on a keypad. She didn't know how Mr. Willet could bear to visit his wife in a locked wing every day, but when she had once asked Min about this, her grandmother had replied that you would be surprised what you can get used to.

"But she's locked in!" Flora had exclaimed.

"She's safe."

"She's Mr. Willet's *wife*. How can he stand it?"

"What's his choice?"

"She could live with him in his apartment."

Min had shaken her head. "No. She needs full-time care. Mr. Willet can't manage that."

"I know," Flora had said. But every time she punched in the code and waited for the door to click open, she felt a pang like a jolt of electricity delivered to the core of her body.

Flora greeted the nurses at their station and walked along the quiet corridor to a door with a wreath of dried roses on it. She had made the wreath herself and given it to Mrs. Willet on her birthday. She hadn't wrapped it, since Mrs. Willet didn't understand about opening presents. And she hadn't expected a thank-you, since Mrs. Willet rarely spoke. But she had been surprised and pleased when Mrs. Willet had looked at the wreath and smiled broadly. Later, Mr. Willet had hung it on her door.

Flora peeked into the room. "Mrs. Willet?" she said softly, and saw that the old woman was snoozing in her armchair. She hesitated and stepped back into the hallway, then changed her mind and entered the room anyway. She stood for nearly a minute watching Mrs. Willet sleep. Mrs. Willet's face was peaceful, but her hands, fingers interlaced, bounced up and down in her lap. Her eyes remained closed, though, so finally Flora whispered, "See you next week," and tiptoed away.

She made her way to Mr. Willet's apartment then and found Mr. Willet and Mr. Pennington deep in conversation.

"Am I interrupting something?" asked Flora.

"Not at all," said Mr. Pennington.

Mr. Willet added, "We're just a couple of old geezers." He held up a T-shirt. "Look what my niece sent me."

Flora peered at the writing on the front of the shirt. "'Old Geezer,'" she read, and personally thought that the shirt was not a very nice gift but refrained from saying so.

Ten minutes later, Flora and Mr. Pennington and Mr. Willet said their good-byes, and soon Flora was on her way home. One of the nice things, she thought, about being a working girl was that it kept her mind off of herself. And off of Ruby and their fight.

Min had not returned from Needle and Thread when Flora stepped into the Row House, so Flora checked her assignments, realized she could do all her homework after dinner, and set about preparing the meal. She chopped vegetables for a salad, decided to bake potatoes, and put one of Min's casseroles in the oven. She was feeding King Comma and Daisy when Ruby came home. Wordlessly, Ruby began to set the table, and she was just finishing up when the front door opened. Moments later, Min appeared in the kitchen.

"Oh, wonderful, Ruby. Thank you for setting the table."

"You're welcome."

"Hi, honey," Min said to Flora, and kissed her cheek. "How was Three Oaks?"

"It was fine." Flora waited for Min to comment on dinner, which everyone could smell. When she didn't, Flora finally said, "I started dinner." The problem with having been responsible and helpful your entire life, Flora reflected, was that eventually people took you for granted. On the other hand, if Ruby so much as blotted up a spot on the counter, Min practically bought her a ticket to Disney World.

"Well, dinner," said Ruby dismissively. "I think that's a casserole *you* made, isn't it, Min?"

Flora fumed but held her tongue until dinner had been eaten and the kitchen tidied. The moment Min stepped out for an evening visit with Mr. Pennington, Flora raged up the stairs to her sister's room. The door was ajar, and Flora pushed it open with a bang. "Okay, that's *it*!" she exclaimed.

Ruby was sitting on her bed, her math book open beside her, a comic book spread across her knees. When the door flew open, she jumped and the comic slid to the floor. "Hey!" cried Ruby. "What are you *do*ing?"

"Listen, Little Miss Perfect, you have to tell Min about the owl. Now."

"What? *Why?*"

"Because I can't take one more second of what you're doing to Min."

"What am I doing to her?"

"You're going out of your way to make her think you've changed —"

"I *have* changed."

"But you haven't told her the reason you've changed. I think she might like to know the reason, don't you?"

Ruby glared at Flora. "What do you mean?"

"I mean that you have to tell Min the truth. You can't keep covering this up. It's too big."

Ruby shrugged at her sister, popped her gum, and retrieved her comic book.

"I'm not kidding, Ruby. Tell her the truth. Or else."

"Or else what?"

"Or else I'll tell her myself."

Ruby's eyes widened. "You're not going to do that! You'd just be a tattletale."

It was Flora's turn to shrug. "It's up to you. Either you tell her or I will." She looked at her watch. "Min said she'll be back in half an hour."

"Wait, Flora. Don't tell her. Please. I'll do it. I promise. Only . . . I need time to figure out what I'm going to say to her. And not half an hour. More than that."

"How much more?"

"A month?" said Ruby in a small voice.

"I'll give you two weeks. Period. The end."

Higglety Pigglety Pop

Bill Willet sat in an armchair in the living room of his apartment at Three Oaks. He stared across the room at the couch where he had tossed the loathsome Old Geezer T-shirt. He couldn't imagine what had possessed his niece to send it to him. She must have thought it was funny. But there really wasn't anything funny about old geezers, particularly when you were eighty years old and had no hair and lived in . . . Well, let's face it, as nice as Three Oaks was, and no matter what you called it, it was still an old people's home.

Mr. Willet sat and stared. The more he stared at the T-shirt, the more he hated it. And, he realized, the less he felt like an old geezer. Maybe *that* was what was wrong with the T-shirt. If he wore it, then people would think he really was an old geezer, but eighty or not, hair or not, and home or not, he didn't feel like he was eighty. And he certainly didn't feel like an old geezer. He was just Bill Willet, who at birth had been given the slightly unfortunate name of William Willet. He could be Bill, who was three, or Bill, who was thirty, or Bill, who was leaning pretty hard on eighty-one.

On the other hand, he walked with a cane and needed a hearing aid in his left ear, neither of which helped much where the old geezer image was concerned.

Mr. Willet sighed. The day was absolutely gorgeous. It was the kind of spring weather that once would have beckoned him and his wife to the backyard of their Row House to work in the flower beds, but for some reason this memory didn't cheer him. He stood up and opened the door to his terrace. He sat on the squeaky wicker chair and breathed in the scent of lilacs. His neighbor in the apartment below had a patio with a garden that he worked in nearly year-round. Mr. Willet longed to have a garden of his own again. He longed to have a job. He longed to take Mary Lou's hand and walk the paths in front of Three Oaks with her. He longed to tell her he loved her and hear her say the words back to him.

"Pity party," he said aloud, standing up. "That's what I'm having. A pity party."

He strode back into his apartment, closing the sliding door behind him with just a bit too much force. Across the room, Sweetie jumped at the noise, leaped up from the Old Geezer T-shirt, where he had settled for a nap, and fled into the kitchen, tail fat.

"Sorry, Sweetie," called Mr. Willet.

He sat in the armchair again. Well, this was some exciting morning he was having. Eat breakfast, sit in a chair, sit in another chair, sit in the first chair again. Maybe I'm an old geezer after all, he thought.

He continued to sit there until, for no reason he could figure out, the title of a children's book popped into his head: *Higglety Pigglety Pop!* Where had that come from?

After a while, Mr. Willet let out a long sigh. He could add that to his exciting list of things to do: eat breakfast, sit, sigh, sit again, sigh again.

"Enough is enough," he said at last. "Sweetie, where are you? I'm sorry I scared you. I'm going out." He found Sweetie crouching on the kitchen counter, returned him to the Old Geezer shirt, put on his jacket, and reached for his cane, which was leaning by the front door.

Mr. Willet stumped along the hallway. He realized he was walking in rhythm to the words *higglety pigglety pop*.

Higglety pigglety pop. Higglety pigglety pop.

He reached the elevator and pressed the button. As he was riding to the ground floor, he suddenly remembered the rest of the title of the children's book: *Higglety Pigglety Pop! There Must Be More to Life.*

"I'll say," he muttered. He checked his watch. It was only 9:40. The day stretched ahead of him. Mr. Willet suppressed a third sigh as he stepped off the elevator.

He began the walk through the corridors of Three Oaks to Mary Lou's room.

"Morning, Bill!" called his friend Evie as Mr. Willet passed her in the hallway. "A fine day, isn't it?"

"Perfect weather. I'm going to take Mary Lou for a walk."

"Good morning, Mr. Willet!" called Dee from the front desk.

"Good morning." Mr. Willet gave her a wave.

He passed the coffee shop, the gift shop, the library, and the exercise center. Ordinarily, these familiar sights made him smile. Today he passed them stonily. He reached the keypad by the door to the wing where his wife now lived and punched in the code.

Before the door had even clicked shut behind him, he saw Mary Lou. And as he walked across the lounge, what he saw was a very young Mary Lou: Mary Lou, with smooth strong hands and an unlined face, studying a textbook, then looking up at Mr. Willet with clear eyes and smiling in pleasure at the sight of him.

But when he stood before her wheelchair, the hand that he reached for was creased, the bones of her fingers bulging painfully in impossible directions. And the eyes that she turned to him were blank, as if he were looking into the eyes of a doll.

"Good morning, honey," he said. He realized that her hand was shaking.

"Is it . . . today . . . here?" she asked vaguely.

"Yes!" exclaimed Mr. Willet. "It's today, and it's ten minutes to ten in the morning. Would you like to take a walk?"

Mrs. Willet glanced down the hallway and lowered her voice to a whisper. "He doesn't know where he's going," she said conspiratorially. (The hallway was empty.)

"He doesn't?" replied Mr. Willet.

"No."

"Well, that's all right. Let's take a walk, shall we? It's a beautiful day."

Mr. Willet didn't expect an answer. He turned to an attendant. "Mary Lou and I are going to take a walk outside," he told him. "We'll have lunch in the coffee shop before I bring her back."

"Enjoy the day" was the reply.

Mr. Willet draped a sweater around his wife's shoulders, and soon he was pushing her chair through the main entrance of Three Oaks and along a sidewalk.

"Look at the gardens," he said. "Everything's blooming away. Narcissus, daffodils, bleeding hearts, grape hyacinths. Remember our gardens?" There was no answer from the wheelchair, so Mr. Willet continued. "Pretty soon the azaleas and the rhododendrons will be in bloom, too."

The hands clasped in Mrs. Willet's lap bounced up and down, and her left foot began to wag back and forth. Mr. Willet paused by a wooden bench, set the brakes on the wheelchair, sat heavily on the bench, and gazed at the gardens.

Flora had mentioned the gardens to him the day before when she'd come to his apartment. "They look like English gardens," she had said. "Or what I think English gardens look like. I've never actually seen one. Have you?"

Mr. Willet had smiled. "Yes. Mary Lou and I took several trips to England. One of them was a tour through the Cotswolds in spring. We saw beautiful gardens."

"Lucky," said Flora, who had stopped just short of embarrassingly saying, "Lucky duck." Then she had turned to Mr. Pennington and added, "Have you seen a real English garden?"

"I have."

"I wish I could get out and see the world," Flora had replied. And then she had done something unexpected. She had turned back to Mr. Willet and said, "I think *you* need to get out and see the world again." Moments later, she had gathered up her things and left with Mr. Pennington.

Now, why had Flora said that? wondered Mr. Willet. She hadn't told Mr. Pennington that *he* needed to see the world. And Mr. Willet hadn't mentioned anything about feeling restless or like a useless old geezer. But as he sat by the gardens and recalled his conversation with Flora, who was an unusual girl, and as the phrase "there must be more to life" ran around and around in his head, an idea came to him.

As soon as he had finished lunch with Mary Lou and walked her back to her room, he settled himself in the Three Oaks library and began to look up information on trips for seniors. He found walking tours (those must be for people who were a little less senior than he was) and cruises (he had never been a big fan of boats) and trips to places that seemed a bit too exotic. And then he found a description of a bus tour through the Cotswolds.

"A bus tour," he murmured. "I could manage that."

He copied down some information, a phone number, and a web address. He wasn't sure how he would feel about traveling without Mary Lou but — *higglety pigglety pop* — he was going to see the Cotswolds again. Surely he would meet some other nice seniors on the trip. Maybe he would even invite Mr. Pennington to go along. He would bring his camera with him. And he would take a photo of an English garden for Flora.

CHAPTER II

One Day at a Time

Hilary Nelson walked slowly down the stairs from her apartment to the door that opened onto Main Street. Spencer ran noisily ahead of her and jumped down the last three steps, landing with a thud. He flung the door open and announced, "It's summer!"

It was April 30th, and not particularly warm, but Spencer had convinced his parents that he could wear shorts that day.

"Come *on*, Hilary!" he called, holding the door open for her with his foot.

"I'm coming." Hilary felt grouchy but tried not to show it, since it wasn't Spencer's fault. She increased her speed by an infinitesimal amount, edged through the door, and stood outside the window of the diner.

Hilary and Ruby had worked hard during the past few weeks to help improve things at the Marquis. It had been Hilary's idea to hold a poster contest for the kids in their class and to display the posters in the window of the Marquis.

"Get it?" she had told Ruby. "People will come by to look at their kids' posters and then they'll stay for dinner or ice cream or something."

Ruby's idea had been that the person who won the poster contest would have a sandwich named after him — or her. Sadly, she had lost the contest to Robert Swenson, who was new in class.

"What kind of a boring sandwich will The Robert be?" Ruby had grumbled to Hilary the morning after the judging of the contest. And would she *never* see The Ruby up there on the sandwich board?

"Mom and Dad will think of something interesting," Hilary had replied confidently.

Hilary and Ruby had also made paper flowers for the vases on the tables in the diner and spent Hilary's money (Ruby seemed to be short on cash) on boxes of crayons so that kids who came to the Marquis could color on the paper place mats.

"It's like we have little elves," commented Hilary's mother the morning after the crayons appeared.

Ruby and Hilary had been working very hard indeed — and Hilary was somewhat poorer than she had been at the beginning of the month — but it was worth everything if they could save the diner.

"I can't even think about moving back to Boston," Hilary had said several times to Ruby during April.

And now it was the last day of the Nelsons'

experimental month. That evening her parents would decide whether to stay in Camden Falls, at least for a while longer, or join the ranks of the families who had had to move on for one reason or another.

Hilary had woken up with butterflies in her stomach. They had stayed with her during breakfast and they were with her now as she stood before the window. She simply could not bear to leave her new home. It would be one thing if her family could pack up and go back to their old house in Boston. But that wasn't possible. And anyway, it wasn't the point. The point was that Hilary had fallen in love with Camden Falls. She loved Main Street, even if it was on the shabby side. She loved her teeny room in the apartment over the diner. She loved Camden Falls Elementary, and her teacher, and walking to school with Ruby and the kids from the Row Houses, and going to concerts at the community center, and the fact that she lived across the street from the library. She truly did not know what she would do if her parents decided the diner was a failure. She hoped that at the very least they would let her and Spencer finish out the school year before they moved (again).

Hilary cupped her hands around her face and peered through a gap between two posters in the window. She could see her father moving around in the Marquis. Her mother, she knew, would be downstairs in just a few minutes, and soon the diner would open for breakfast.

"Come *on*!" called Spencer again.

Hilary followed her brother to the corner, turned onto Dodds Lane, and looked ahead to Aiken Avenue. Ruby, the Morris kids, Olivia's brothers, and Cole Hamilton were waiting in a noisy group.

"There they are!" called Jack Walter, pointing at Hilary and Spencer.

"Hurry up!" added Mathias Morris.

"What are they in such a rush for?" Hilary asked her brother.

"We want to play softball before the first bell," Spencer called over his shoulder, and he and all the kids except Ruby took off down the street.

Hilary approached Ruby slowly.

"So today's the day," said Ruby when Hilary finally caught up with her.

"Yup."

"Do you have *any* idea what's going to happen?"

"Nope."

"Your parents haven't given you a single clue?"

"Nope."

"But you'll know tonight?"

"Yup." Hilary expelled a sigh. Then she added, "You didn't tell anyone, did you?"

"No!" Ruby was in enough trouble as it was, and she knew better than to leak Hilary's secret and become known as a blabbermouth in addition to everything else.

When they reached school, Ruby said, "Want to play softball?"

Hilary shook her head. "But you play if you want to."

"What are you going to do?"

"Nothing. Just wait." Hilary stood in the yard of Camden Falls Elementary and took a good long look at her school. It was smaller than the one she had attended in Boston, a fact which at first she had found troubling. She remembered saying to her mother, "What are Spencer and I supposed to *do* in this tiny little place?" Then she had toured CFE and found that her dinky new school had an impressive library, a sprawling playground, a cafeteria, *and* an auditorium.

"This isn't so bad," Hilary had confessed.

In fact, fifth grade with Mrs. Caldwell had turned out to be Hilary's best school year ever.

"Where will you wait?" asked Ruby now.

"In our classroom."

"Can I wait with you?"

Hilary shrugged. "Sure."

She and Ruby made their way to Mrs. Caldwell's room (they were the only ones there), and Hilary sat at her desk and looked around at the bulletin boards, and leftover science fair projects, and the aquarium containing tropical fish, and the turtle Ava Longyear had brought in but that Mrs. Caldwell insisted would have to be returned to his natural habitat that afternoon.

"You're kind of acting like this is the last time you're going to see our room," said Ruby after a few moments.

Hilary shrugged again.

"Well, even if your parents decide to sell the diner, you aren't going to move *tomorrow*." Ruby sounded just the teensiest bit cross.

"I don't know when we might move," Hilary replied.

Ruby said she was going to go outside and play softball after all, so Hilary was left alone, mentally bidding farewell to room 5A.

One of the best things about Mrs. Caldwell, Hilary thought, was that she was full of surprises, and that day brought yet another surprise.

"Class," said Mrs. Caldwell when everyone was settled at their desks and the morning business had been attended to, "we've had an exciting year. Last week I was thinking about our year and all that we've done — the things we've studied, the trips we've taken, the science fair, our correspondence with our pen pals in Florida — and I thought it might be nice to have a program for your families on the last day of school. It would be an opportunity to share our year with —"

Ruby's hand shot up before Mrs. Caldwell had finished speaking.

"Yes, Ruby?"

"What kind of a program? A play?"

"As a matter of fact I am thinking of a play — just a small one that we can put on here in our room."

"When are auditions?"

Mrs. Caldwell smiled. "No auditions. We're going to put your names in a hat and assign roles that way."

"Oh." Ruby scowled.

"And we're going to do that right now. We'll need a narrator — that's the biggest role — and ten people to tell our guests about our projects, and a small group to perform a song."

To Hilary's delight, her teacher produced a hat from under her desk and began pulling slips of paper out of it and writing names on the board. When Mrs. Caldwell said, "And for the narrator . . . Hilary Nelson," Hilary's eyes opened wide.

Once again, Ruby's hand shot in the air. "Mrs. Caldwell, did you know that Hilary might —" Ruby started to say before she glanced at Hilary, closed her mouth, and turned red. "Um, never mind."

"What?" said Mrs. Caldwell, looking puzzled. She glanced at Hilary.

"It's okay," Hilary told her, even though she dreaded having to walk into school the next morning and tell her teacher that she'd be in Boston on the last day of school. Mrs. Caldwell would have to draw names again to find a new narrator and then switch everyone else around.

Twice during the afternoon Hilary almost asked Mrs. Caldwell if they could have a private conference. She planned to suggest that Ruby be given the role of narrator, since she wanted it so badly. But she was afraid she would somehow jinx her parents' decision.

On the other hand, accepting the role of narrator when she probably wouldn't be able to keep it was kind of selfish.

Hilary couldn't figure out *what* to do, so she did nothing.

She left school that afternoon with a headache — and a heavier heart than she could have imagined. When she entered the diner, which she was pleased to see was fairly crowded, she ran to her father. "Did you and Mom make a decision?"

"Not yet, honey. We've been busy today. We'll look at everything tonight, I promise."

The butterflies returned.

That evening, as soon as the diner had closed and the Nelsons had eaten dinner in their apartment, Hilary's parents sat down at the living room table, which was strewn with papers. They sat together for a full hour, murmuring, studying bank statements, and sifting through receipts. Hilary was completely unable to concentrate on her homework. She sat and watched her parents, her heart thudding, her headache in full swing.

At one point Spencer leaned into the room and said to Hilary, "They could probably work faster if you weren't staring at them."

Hilary reluctantly moved to her bedroom, where she sat at her desk and thought darkly about living in her grandparents' house, sharing a bedroom with not only Spencer but her parents. Or sleeping on a couch in the living room. Then she pictured herself approaching Mrs. Caldwell's desk the next morning and breaking the news to her about the class program. Mrs. Caldwell had never gotten angry with Hilary, or with any of her students, but maybe she would get a disappointed grown-up look on her face, one that said, "You've let me down. Now we have to draw names again and start over."

"Hilary! Spencer!" she heard her mother call from the living room.

Hilary shot up so quickly that she knocked her chair over. She didn't bother to right it. She tore down the hall to the living room, bumping into Spencer on the way, and stood breathlessly in front of her parents.

"Are we moving?" she asked.

Spencer stood at her side.

Her parents looked at each other. Then they smiled.

"We're staying," her father said.

"At least for the time being," her mother added.

"Yes!" cried Hilary. "Yes, yes, yes!"

Spencer let out a whoop. "Are we rich?"

Hilary's mother laughed. "Far from it. But we're doing okay."

"And that's the best we can ask for right now," added her father.

"Did I help?" asked Hilary. "You know, the crayons, the poster contest?"

"Definitely," said her parents in unison.

"I'm going to call Ruby!" Hilary made a dash for the phone. On the way she called over her shoulder, "Oh, by the way, our class is putting on a program on the last day of school. You're invited. I'm going to be the narrator!"

CHAPTER 12

The Perfect Dog

Nikki sat on a stool behind the counter at Sincerely Yours, feeling very grown-up. She liked to pretend that she worked there. Robby worked there part-time and Olivia worked there once a week or so, and Nikki marveled at the way they talked to customers and wrapped packages and stocked the shelves.

But Nikki didn't work there, and on this particular afternoon, Olivia wasn't working there, either. The girls were there because they were avoiding Flora and Ruby.

"How long do you think their fight can possibly go on?" Olivia asked. She glanced around, slipped a plastic glove on one hand, reached into the candy display, and withdrew two chocolates.

"No sneaking food!" said Robby loudly from across the store. "You have to pay! It's the rule."

Olivia blushed, and she and Nikki ate the chocolates in a big hurry.

Nikki wiped her mouth guiltily. "I have no idea how long it'll go on. It's been going on forever already." She paused. "Maybe they'll *never* make up. Do you think that could actually happen?"

Olivia shrugged. "The whole thing is awful. Every time I'm with Ruby she asks me about Flora, and every time I'm with Flora she asks me about Ruby. You'd never know they live in the same house. Plus, it's really uncomfortable. They're putting me in a bad position."

Nikki looked longingly at the trays of chocolates. "They're doing the same thing to me. I finally had to tell Flora I wouldn't talk to her about Ruby and vice versa. But that feels, I don't know, artificial. And also like I'm not being a good friend."

"On the other hand," said Olivia thoughtfully, "they won't tell us what the fight is about. That doesn't really seem fair."

"I guess it isn't our business, though."

"No, but if they won't tell us about it, then they shouldn't ask us stuff."

Nikki grunted in frustration.

"Why can't things just be like before?" Olivia said, more loudly than she had intended, and two customers turned to look at her. She lowered her voice. "There were four of us. We were best friends. It was simple."

"As simple as friendship can be." Nikki eyed the chocolates again. "Can we have more if I pay for them?"

"Yes!" called Robby.

Nikki chose two more chocolates and handed one to Olivia, along with a dollar bill.

"Thanks," said Olivia. She let her gaze wander out the window to Main Street. "Let's not talk about this anymore," she said finally. "I mean, not right now."

"Okay. But you know we're going to have to do something about it eventually," replied Nikki.

"Maybe, maybe not."

The next afternoon, Nikki had just arrived at Sheltering Arms when she heard someone say, "The first vans are on their way."

"What vans?" Nikki asked Greta, another volunteer.

"There's a big rescue going on. At some farm — well, not really a farm — with all these dogs and puppies —"

"A puppy mill?" Nikki asked, and felt her stomach drop.

"I'm not sure. Someone called Animal Control to report bad odors and lots of barking coming from their neighbors' property. The officers made a call and found dozens of dogs and puppies living in tiny, cramped cages with almost no food, empty water bowls, you know."

Unfortunately, Nikki did know. She'd seen it before.

Greta made a face and then continued. "Apparently, there are quite a few dead dogs, too."

Nikki closed her eyes briefly.

"And a lot of the dogs are sick — eye infections, tumors, heartworm. One even has fur that's so matted he can't see. They're going to have to shave him completely. His eyesight is probably already damaged, though."

"Oh, no," said Nikki. "Are *any* of the dogs okay?"

The volunteer held her hands out. "Don't know. Maybe. There are two mom dogs with litters of newborn puppies. Maybe the puppies can be saved, at least."

"How many dogs are there altogether? They aren't all coming here, are they?"

"I haven't heard the total, but no, they aren't all coming here. There are too many. Some will go to the SPCA, some will go to the shelter in Mechanicsville. I think I heard Harriet say that eighteen of them are coming here."

"Okay," said Nikki.

She stepped into the restroom and stood at the sink for a few moments. She needed to have a chat with herself. If you are going to work at a shelter, she said sternly (in her head), you have to get used to this. You have to have a strong backbone. She remembered something Harriet had told her: "Don't get callous, but don't get overwhelmed, either. You need a kind heart for this work, but you also need to be able to separate yourself from the cruelty you'll see. It's a fine balance."

"Okay," she said again. And she stepped out into the lobby of Sheltering Arms.

The first van arrived five minutes later.

Nikki stood by the front doors and watched as Ms. Hewitt, who ran Sheltering Arms, and Harriet and several of the other adult workers unloaded six crates from the back. She tried to peep into the crates as they were carried past her.

The crates had just been set inside when another van arrived. Sheltering Arms took on the feel of a hospital emergency room. Volunteers hustled back and forth, vets peered into the crates, Ms. Hewitt gave orders, doors slammed, phone calls were made.

"Wow," said Nikki softly as she watched the activity, eyes wide.

By the time the third van had arrived and been unloaded, Nikki wasn't even sure where to stand.

"You look lost," someone said, and Nikki turned around to find Harriet behind her.

"I don't exactly know what to do," she admitted.

The dogs with the most serious problems had been hustled into examining rooms and were being seen to by the veterinarians and vet techs.

"Come with me," said Harriet, smiling and extending her hand. "Let's take a look at the dogs who aren't in any immediate danger." She led Nikki to a room that was lined from one end to the other, and on both sides of an aisle, with large pens. It was a room for dogs who weren't ready for adoption yet, dogs who needed to be treated and observed first.

"Okay, let's see what we have so far," said Harriet.

The dogs were still being settled into their new quarters, and Nikki heard whining and whimpering and also a few angry barks.

"I don't blame you," she said to a skinny dog who had retreated to the farthest corner of his pen. She could see all his ribs, could actually count them from where she was standing. His eyes were runny and red and he was keeping one of his front feet off the ground.

"His foot looks swollen," Nikki said to Harriet in a low voice.

"One of the vets will look at him later this afternoon," Harriet replied.

"He's terrified," Nikki added.

"But you know how quickly some of the dogs come around."

Nikki nodded. She did.

At one end of the room, separated from the other dogs by two empty pens, was a nursing mom dog. Nikki crept toward the cage and peered inside. The dog was lying on her side, five tiny puppies wiggling against her body, snuffling as they drank. The mom watched Nikki and tipped her tail hesitantly.

"Hey!" Nikki cried softly. "This dog looks okay. So do her puppies. They just need a little cleaning up."

She walked from pen to pen, glancing in at frightened dogs, dirty dogs, and dogs with matted fur. Most of them had slunk to the backs of their cages and watched her warily.

"Do you want to help me feed them?" asked Harriet.

"Definitely!" Nikki said, and began filling bowls with chow and water. When she reached the pen nearest the door, she stopped. A fuzzy brown dog was sitting at the very front of the pen.

"He's smiling at me!" Nikki exclaimed. "Look, Harriet. Really. He's smiling."

Harriet laughed. "He seems sweet."

Nikki stood near the dog but kept her hands at her sides. "Hi, dog," she said.

The dog flicked his tail up and down and then set it sweeping back and forth across the floor.

"You're awfully friendly," said Nikki.

The dog put his paws on the pen and stood on his hind legs. His ears perked forward, his tail now wagged with great enthusiasm, and his grin widened. He looked hopefully at Nikki.

"How old do you think he is?" Nikki asked Harriet.

"The vet will have to take a look at his teeth, but I don't think he's a puppy. He might even be six or seven."

"Huh," said Nikki. "Just the right age for a dog for Mr. Pennington."

"Now, don't go getting your hopes up," Harriet cautioned her. "We don't know a thing about him. The vet hasn't seen him yet. He could be two years old and have heartworm."

"We know he's friendly," said Nikki.

"He *was* very gentle when I gave him his food."

"I'm going to call Mr. Pennington tonight."

"*After* he's been seen by a vet. Truly, Nikki. He has a ways to go before he's adoptable."

"I know. It's just that he's sweet and friendly like Jacques was, and he's not a puppy, and also he's the right size — not too big."

Nikki couldn't wait until Harriet dropped her off at her house that evening. By the time she had left Sheltering Arms, the friendly just-right-for-Mr.-Pennington dog had been examined by a vet and found to be healthy except for a bad case of fleas, a mild infection in his left eye, and some suspicious wounds on his back. Everything was treatable, the dog continued to seem amiable, he was cooperative when being examined by the vet, and to top things off, his age was estimated at five.

"Mr. Pennington!" Nikki cried the moment he answered his phone. "Guess what!" She tried to slow down and tell him about the rescue in a calm and organized manner. She wound up by saying, "The vet thinks he's about five years old."

"Could —" Mr. Pennington started to ask.

But Nikki had thought of something else. "He needs to be neutered before you can adopt him. And they want to work with him to make absolutely sure he isn't aggressive and that he gets along with kids and other dogs, so you won't be able to adopt him right away, but —"

"Could I go to the shelter and meet him?"

"Definitely. I'll give you Ms. Hewitt's number."

"Thank you, Nikki."

CHAPTER 13

Variety

Rudy Pennington didn't wait long to meet the friendly dog at the shelter. In fact, the moment he ended his phone conversation with Nikki, he clicked his phone back on and called Ms. Hewitt. But he got a recording saying that Sheltering Arms was closed for the evening and would reopen the next morning.

"Darn," said Mr. Pennington aloud, but he was feeling quite cheerful. He opened a cupboard in his kitchen and checked the shelf where he had kept Jacques's food. Four cans were left, as well as half a bag of dry food. "Excellent!" he said. Whistling, he opened the closet in the front hall and peered into the bag in which he had stowed Jacques's leash, collar, toys, brush, and dishes. He examined them one by one. The collar was fraying, but the leash looked fine, as did the brush, the dishes, and most of the toys.

A trip to the Cheshire Cat was probably in order. He would need another collar, and . . . maybe his new dog would like a bed. Jacques had preferred the couch, but maybe Mr. Pennington should buy a nice fleecy bed for . . . He paused. He was getting ahead of himself. He didn't even know whether the dog was available, or whether he would be chosen as the person to adopt him. First things first. Talk to Ms. Hewitt.

The recording at Sheltering Arms had said to call back after 8:30 a.m. So the next morning, Mr. Pennington waited until his kitchen clock said 8:31 and then he picked up his phone. Half an hour later he was driving through the countryside to Sheltering Arms, on his way to meet the dog with the fleas and the eye infection and the wounds that Nikki thought would be perfect for him.

He was greeted at the front desk by Harriet, and after he had answered several questions, Harriet took him to an outdoor pen. She left him there and returned a few minutes later leading a fuzzy brown dog who was biting at his leash in a playful manner.

"It's probably his first time on a leash," Harriet remarked.

She released the dog and he approached Mr. Pennington at once.

"May I pat him?" he asked.

Harriet nodded, and Mr. Pennington extended his hand. The dog sniffed it, then stepped forward and sat down on Mr. Pennington's feet.

"I think he likes you," said Harriet, smiling.

"The feeling is mutual." Mr. Pennington studied the dog. "What on earth are you?" he asked, running his hands along the dog's back. "You look a little like a terrier and also a little like a poodle."

"Really?" said Harriet. "I was thinking he looks sort of like a greyhound. And maybe a basset hound. Look how long his ears are."

Harriet brought Mr. Pennington a chair then, and he sat in the sunshine while the dog wandered around, chasing insects and sniffing the grass, and finally sat on Mr. Pennington's feet again.

After a while, Mr. Pennington said, "So . . . where do we go from here?"

"Why don't you come inside and fill out an application. I'm sure it will be approved. We'll work with the dog until he's healthy and ready for adoption, and then he'll be all yours," Harriet replied.

Two days later, Mr. Pennington returned to Sheltering Arms for another visit with the dog and to meet with Ms. Hewitt, who told him his application had been approved.

"He's a great dog," said Ms. Hewitt. "He's lucky he wasn't in worse shape. And it's a miracle that he has such a sweet disposition. Heaven only knows how he's been treated."

"I wonder what he's a mix of," said Mr. Pennington.

"He looks like a beagle," replied Ms. Hewitt. "And I can see some Lab, too."

Over the weekend, Mr. Pennington returned again, this time bringing Min, Flora, and Ruby along.

"Oh, he's so cute!" cried Ruby when she saw him. "What is he? A boxer?"

"A boxer!" exclaimed Flora, although Mr. Pennington noted that Flora carefully avoided her sister's eyes. "No way. He's one of those dogs in the taco commercials."

"You think?" said Min. "I see golden retriever in him, definitely. Just like Daisy."

The following week, Mr. Pennington drove Nikki to Sheltering Arms for her afternoon of volunteering, and he stayed to visit his dog.

"I think you should name him Marmaduke," announced Nikki.

"Marmaduke? Why?"

"He has a head like a Great Dane. He looks like that cartoon dog."

"Huh," replied Mr. Pennington. "A Great Dane. Well, I don't know."

"Anyway, he's making wonderful progress. Ms. Hewitt said so. He doesn't show any food aggression and he's calm around other dogs. And he's learning to walk on a leash. Oh, and he's pretty much house-broken, too."

"Well, that's good news," remarked Mr. Pennington.

"I'll have to check with Ms. Hewitt," Nikki went on, "but I think you can take him home after he's been neutered. We can find out today if that's been sched-uled. I know the volunteers are still working on his social skills, even though he seems to be doing well."

The next day, Mr. Pennington returned for another visit. He sat on a lawn chair in the outdoor pen, the dog at his feet. A butterfly swooped by and the dog leaped for it. Then he smiled at Mr. Pennington and jumped into his lap.

"Well, what do you know. This is the first time you've climbed in my lap."

The dog grinned again, turned around, and settled down, his feet hanging over Mr. Pennington's knees.

"I think," said Mr. Pennington, "that if you were a cat you'd be purring now."

The dog glanced at him and then fell asleep.

"I have to decide on a name for you, boy, and it has to be just the right name. Jacques was the right name for my other dog, but I haven't thought of the right name for you. It can't be a cute name like Lucky or Sunny or Winky. Pardon me, but as wonderful as you are, a cute name doesn't suit you. I'll have to keep thinking."

After that, Mr. Pennington fell asleep briefly him-self, so he and the dog napped in the sunshine. They awoke when Harriet turned up to bring the dog back to his pen.

"Good news," she said. "His surgery has been sched-uled for tomorrow. You can take him home on Saturday."

"Adoption Day," said Mr. Pennington happily. "Thank you, Harriet. I might bring a few people along for the special event."

On Saturday morning, Rudy Pennington arrived at Sheltering Arms with Min, Flora, and Ruby. Nikki met them at the door.

"Surprise!" she said. "I wanted to be here for Adoption Day, too."

"How's the dog?" asked Flora.

Ms. Hewitt stepped out of her office. "Nicely recovered from his surgery," she replied. "He is one wonderful dog. And one lucky dog."

"I think I'm one lucky human," said Mr. Pennington.

"Everyone, wait here," said Nikki suddenly. "I'll be right back."

A few minutes later, Nikki returned with the dog, who was wearing a large red bow around his neck. "Ta-dah!" she said.

Mr. Pennington laughed. "Very fetching."

Nikki dropped the leash, the dog looked around at the group of people in the lobby, and then he trotted directly to Mr. Pennington.

"Hi, buddy!" Mr. Pennington stooped down and gave the dog a hug.

"Is that his name?" asked Ruby. "Buddy?"

"Absolutely not. I haven't thought of his name yet."

"How about Cotton?" suggested Ruby.

"Jacques the Second," suggested Flora.

"Beau," suggested Nikki.

Mr. Pennington kept shaking his head. "The right name will come to me in good time."

"Well," spoke up Ms. Hewitt, "all that remains is for you to sign the official adoption form and then you can take your new companion home."

Mr. Pennington stood at the desk and signed several papers.

"He's all yours," Ms. Hewitt said then.

Mr. Pennington, Min, Flora, Ruby, and the nameless dog piled into Mr. Pennington's car and were soon on their way back to Aiken Avenue.

"I think he likes riding in the car," remarked Ruby.

The dog was sitting in the backseat, a serious expression on his face, watching the scenery fly by.

They drove down Main Street.

"This is Camden Falls," Mr. Pennington called over his shoulder. "We'll be taking walks on this street very soon." Mr. Pennington turned onto Aiken Avenue and pulled up in front of the Row Houses. "And here," he went on, "is your new home."

Mr. Pennington parked the car and snapped Jacques's old leash onto the dog's collar. He let him sniff the front lawn. "Welcome home," he said.

Min, Flora, and Ruby stood back and watched the dog's first few moments of his new life.

"What kind of dog *is* he?" asked Flora.

"He's about a million different things," said Ruby.

Mr. Pennington smiled. "That's it! You've just given me the idea for his name."

"What is it?" asked Min.

"Variety. His name is Variety." Mr. Pennington opened his front door. "Come on in and see your house, Variety," he said. And they disappeared inside.

CHAPTER 14

The Perfect Day

Ruby was torn between feeling elated and terrified. She was elated not only because Mr. Pennington had brought Variety home that morning but because she had big plans for the afternoon. She was terrified because her deadline for telling Min the truth about the owl was fast approaching, and she knew Flora would hold her to it. If Ruby didn't tell Min what had happened, then Flora would do it for her.

Ruby tried to tear her mind away from Min and the owl and rigid, unfair Flora. Take one thing at a time, she said to herself. And since she had quite an adventure planned for the afternoon, that's what she turned her thoughts to.

She was glad the weather that May weekend was warm and sunny — what Min would call glorious. In fact, Min had used that very word earlier when they were on their way to Sheltering Arms to bring Variety home.

"A glorious day," Min had said, looking at the clear blue sky. "Simply glorious."

Ruby hoped the weather would remain simply glorious that afternoon. Her plans would work much better in good weather. In fact, if it rained, the whole adventure would probably fall apart.

She thought back to the afternoon two weeks earlier when Aunt Allie had received the phone call that had set the adventure in motion. Ruby had been visiting her aunt and Janie — without Flora — and in fact had been the one to answer the phone when it rang.

"Ruby, could you get that, please?" Allie had asked.

Ruby had been displeased, not because she didn't want to answer the phone, but because Allie had just been about to hand Janie to her. Now Allie took the baby back, saying, "If you can pick up the phone, I'll settle Janie in her swing" (Janie had an indoor swing, of which Ruby was unreasonably jealous) "and then we can trade places."

So Ruby had made a grab for the cordless phone, which she'd found buried on Allie's desk, and said, "Hello? Allie Read's house."

She'd heard the sound of a throat clearing at the other end of the phone. *Ahem.* "Hello?" *Ahem, ahem.* "This is Vincent Barnes." *Ahem.* "Is Allie there?"

"Just a moment, please," Ruby had replied politely. What she'd wanted to do was shout, "Yow! Mr. Barnes is calling you, Aunt Allie!" She wished she and Flora were talking to each other so she could spread the news. On the other hand, it would be sneaky and fun to have such a good secret from her sister.

Ruby had run full speed into the living room, holding the phone at arm's length. She covered the mouthpiece with her hand. "Aunt Allie, it's *Mr. Barnes!*" she hissed. She jerked her thumb across the street in the direction of his house.

"Thank you, Ruby," Aunt Allie had replied, and she took the phone from her so calmly that Ruby wondered if she'd actually heard what she'd said.

"*Mr. Barnes!*" Ruby had repeated, slightly more loudly.

But Aunt Allie was already walking out of the living room, saying, "Hello? Vincent?"

Ruby had looked from Janie, who was now swinging contentedly in the doorway of the living room, to her aunt's disappearing back. She was pretty sure there was some rule about never leaving a baby unattended. Did that only apply to bathtubs? Ruby wasn't sure, but she did not want to miss out on Allie's end of the phone conversation, so keeping an eye on Janie, she'd walked backward down the hall and stood outside her aunt's study. Allie had closed herself inside.

Ruby had considered the situation for less than a second and then plastered her ear against the door.

"Well, that would be lovely," she'd heard her aunt say. "All three of us? Even better. . . . Yes. . . . Yes. . . . Oh, this weekend won't work, though. What about

next weekend? Are you free on Saturday? . . . Okay. . . .
Okay. Great, it's a date."

A date! thought Ruby, who had already been poised
to run, sensing that the conversation was about to end.
Aunt Allie on a *date*! But all three of them? All three
who? What did that mean? It couldn't be an actual
date — not the kind Ruby was thinking of — if more
than two people were involved.

She'd pressed her ear to the door again, hoping for
some clarification, but heard only the sound of footsteps approaching the door. She bolted back to the
living room and had just enough time to position herself in front of the swing before Aunt Allie appeared,
smiling, her face somewhat flushed.

Ruby had looked questioningly at her aunt, but
Allie just continued to smile.

"Good conversation?" Ruby asked.

"Mmm" was the reply.

"So that was Mr. Barnes?"

"Mmm."

"I guess he calls here pretty often."

"Well . . ." Allie said vaguely.

It had taken Ruby nearly half an hour, but eventually she'd learned the details of the phone call. Aunt
Allie and Janie and Mr. Barnes were going to take a
picnic lunch to Tyler Park in two weeks and spend the
afternoon there. Just the three of them.

This was an even better kind of date than Ruby had
imagined. If Janie was going along, it could only mean

that Mr. Barnes wanted to get to know her, too, and *that* could only mean that he was *really* interested in Aunt Allie.

Ruby decided to spy on them.

She simply could not pass up an opportunity to witness the date. The only sad aspect of the affair was not being able to tell Flora about it. As much fun as it would be to keep her sister in the dark about the date, sharing it with her would be even better. But it was out of the question. Ruby was on her own.

After much thinking, she decided to arrive at the park before Allie and Janie and Mr. Barnes got there. That way she could observe the very beginning of their date. So as soon as she had called good-bye to Mr. Pennington and the lucky Variety, she hopped on her bicycle and rode through town to the park. Ruby had never been there by herself and she felt very grown-up as she locked her bike in the rack and strolled along the gravel drive to the information center. She passed between the stone pillars marking the entrance, and there she paused. She needed a good hiding place from which to watch for Aunt Allie, and eventually she positioned herself behind a wooden building marked LATRINES. Not surprisingly, the latrines did not smell good, but Ruby hadn't expected them to, and anyway, sometimes a spy had to make sacrifices.

The park was crowded, with people coming and going — carloads of them. Ruby scanned the people, and while she waited, she decided to come up with a spy name for herself. After a while, she settled on Madame Plush.

Madame Plush stood, shifting from one foot to the other, and holding her nose. At 12:45, she saw a familiar car pull into the parking lot, and she jerked to attention. At the last moment, she remembered that she had stuck a pair of sunglasses in her pocket, and she put them on along with a purple baseball cap that was hanging off one of the belt loops on her jeans.

Holding as still as she was able, she trained her eyes on the car. Aunt Allie stepped out of the driver's seat, Mr. Barnes stepped out of the passenger's seat, Aunt Allie lifted Janie from her seat in the back, and Mr. Barnes began to unload items from the trunk. A cooler, another cooler, two lawn chairs, Janie's stroller, a blanket, Janie's diaper bag . . .

"What on earth?" murmured Madame Plush, before she remembered that Min was always saying that babies don't travel light.

No kidding, thought Madame Plush.

It took quite a while, but finally Aunt Allie and Mr. Barnes managed to gather up Janie and all the other stuff and struggle along the path and through the entrance. They kept dropping things and laughing, and of course it was almost impossible to push the stroller over gravel, which only made them laugh harder.

"Huh," said Madame Plush, thinking that she would not have been so cheerful about the situation.

A few moments later, the messy caravan passed several yards from Madame Plush's hiding place and continued to the banks of Tyler Creek, which ran through the park from the north end to the south.

"This looks like a good spot, doesn't it?" said Aunt Allie, surveying the picnickers and waders and Frisbee players and stopping a little distance from a group of kids Ruby's age who were clearly at a birthday party.

"Perfect," replied Mr. Barnes, and he stopped mid stride and unburdened himself of the chairs, the cooler, and the diaper bag.

Before long, their camp was set up, the chairs arranged side by side in front of the blanket, which Allie and Mr. Barnes had spread out carefully, each holding an end and laughing (again) when the wind tossed it into the air before they could anchor the corners with the coolers and some of Janie's many necessary articles.

At first, Allie, Mr. Barnes, and Janie all sat on the blanket. Allie pulled packages out of the cooler, and Janie played with a spoon and some plastic cups.

"Boring," said Madame Plush aloud, until she realized that Allie and Mr. Barnes were talking — and she couldn't make out a word they were saying.

She edged closer to them, but now she was completely out in the open. If Aunt Allie so much as looked over her shoulder, she would see Ruby standing there plain as day. Ruby eyed the birthday party. Most of the kids were running back and forth between the creek and a large picnic table laden with food. Several were wading; some were walking barefoot along the banks, looking for tadpoles in the water; some were sitting at the table, eating hot dogs; and three were crowded in the shade of a tree, making friendship bracelets. Ruby noticed only four adults, and they were standing in a group, talking earnestly.

She stepped carefully around the girls who were making the bracelets and crept to the banks of the creek. She smiled at another group of kids, then sat down a little apart from them. No one said a word. And Madame Plush, her sunglasses and cap in place, could now hear every word spoken by Allie and Mr. Barnes.

"I'm just a kid at a party," said Ruby to herself. She fiddled with the Velcro on her sneakers, pretended to be fascinated by whatever might be swimming around in Tyler Creek, and listened to the conversation behind her.

"I applied to about a million adoption agencies," Allie was saying to Mr. Barnes. "Paul and I had already applied to adopt a baby from China, and after he left, I investigated other agencies, too."

Uh-oh, thought Madame Plush. It was probably better not to mention past boyfriends when on a date with a new boyfriend.

She strained to hear whatever uncomfortable reply Mr. Barnes might make, but all he said was, "Paul doesn't know what he's missing."

Madame Plush didn't know if he was referring to Janie or Aunt Allie. She risked a quick peek over her shoulder. Allie was smiling broadly at Mr. Barnes and . . . holding his hand.

Ruby's eyes widened. She lost her balance and almost fell in the stream. She grabbed a fistful of tall grass, pulled herself upright, and risked another glance at her aunt. Now Allie was not only holding Mr. Barnes's hand but stroking it.

Ew, thought Madame Plush. Still, this was a good sign. A very good sign. She breathed deeply until her heartbeat had returned to normal. Then she slipped several feet back from the bank of the creek and listened again.

"Are you hungry?" Aunt Allie was saying.

"Starving."

"You watch Janie, then, and I'll get the food ready."

The next time Ruby risked a peek over her shoulder she saw Mr. Barnes cradling a dozing Janie in his arms. "Is she always this good?" he was asking.

Aunt Allie laughed. "Usually. But on the days when she's not in a good mood, she's . . ."

"Horrid," said Allie and Mr. Barnes at the same time, and then they laughed so hard that Ruby wondered what she had missed.

But she didn't care. Madame Plush had unearthed a wonderful secret. Her aunt and Mr. Barnes were becoming more than friends.

Later, as the afternoon grew cool, the birthday party wound down, and Mr. Barnes and Allie loaded up the car. Then they returned to the bank of the creek, where they stood for a few moments, Mr. Barnes holding Janie in one arm, his other arm around Aunt Allie's shoulder.

Madame Plush smiled to herself and walked nonchalantly out of the park with the rest of the party guests.

CHAPTER 15

To Tell the Truth

Ruby knew she was in trouble that night when Flora appeared in her bedroom doorway and just stood there, hand on hip.

"What," said Ruby. She was studying her music for the Children's Chorus performance, which would take place on Monday.

"Time's up," Flora announced.

Ruby looked at her in alarm. "This second?"

"Pretty much."

"I —" Ruby began to say, panicking. But then she frowned. She grabbed a calendar from her desk and began counting squares. "Cheater!" she finally announced, feeling triumphant rather than annoyed. "I knew I had until next week. You said you would give me two weeks, and that was on a Wednesday, and this is Saturday, which is only ten days later. Anyway," Ruby went on, inspired, "I'm going to tell Min on

Monday. I planned it so that I would beat your deadline."

This was not true in the least. (Ruby had planned to tell Min on Monday but not in order to beat the deadline.) She looked meaningfully at Flora anyway. She hoped her sister wouldn't ask her why she had settled on Monday, and she didn't. Flora simply muttered, "Huh," and marched across the hall into her own bedroom.

Ruby sank onto her chair and considered her plan, which was this: to wait until the Children's Chorus performance was over and then tell Min about the owl. Surely, thought Ruby, everyone would rush to her after the concert and congratulate her on her solo. They might even say, "Ruby, we haven't heard your lovely voice in so long!" and, "My land, your voice is even more mature now than it was the last time we heard you." Maybe someone would add, "I think you're about ready for Broadway, Ruby."

If this happened on Monday night, surely Min wouldn't be upset about something as trifling as the replacement (*replacement*) of a broken thing that Min hadn't looked at in months. Ruby would say, "Min, I broke your owl, but I got you another one," and Min would wave off the confession and reply, "Broadway, Ruby. Someone said you're ready for Broadway!"

Ruby wondered if perhaps she could figure out a way for that someone to be Ms. Angelo, the director of the chorus. She hopped out of her chair and grabbed her music again. If there were to be any mention of Broadway, she needed to be at her very best on Monday night.

The evening of the Children's Chorus performance was fine and clear and warm.

"Can we walk to the community center?" Ruby asked Min as they were finishing an early dinner.

Min smiled but shook her head. "It's a lovely night, Ruby, but it'll be dark by the time the performance is over. And tomorrow is a school day. Are you ready? We should leave in about ten minutes."

"I'm ready." Ruby paused. "I mean, I'm *really* ready. I'm ready to go, and I'm all prepared for my solo. No mistakes this time."

Min smiled. "Good for you."

"I hope the concert raises lots of money for the community center," Flora spoke up.

Ruby had almost forgotten that the performance was a benefit for the community center. She tried to put thoughts of Broadway and owls out of her mind. "Yeah, I hope we're sold out tonight," she said hastily.

Later, as Ruby and the other members of the Children's Chorus gathered in a room near the back door of the center to get ready for the show, Ruby watched the audience arrive. She recalled other performances, the great hall decorated for holidays. Tonight there were no decorations, but the hall, which she had peeked into when she and Min and Flora and

Mr. Pennington had arrived, was lit in such a way that the room glowed.

"May I have your attention, please?" Ms. Angelo said to the choir members, clapping her hands. "I'm happy to tell you that we just sold the last ticket for the show, and people are still outside. They're offering to pay for standing-room-only tickets."

Standing room only! SRO. A sold-out performance. This was more than Ruby could have hoped for.

"Quiet now," said Ms. Angelo. "We're on in ten minutes. You need to settle down and start lining up for your entrance."

Later, years later, even, when Ruby remembered this particular evening at the community center, she recalled the faces of her family and her Row House neighbors in the audience, and the smile Ms. Angelo flashed to the chorus members at the end of the performance, and of course the round of applause that followed her solo. The applause went on for so long that Ms. Angelo had to put an end to it. Ruby couldn't stop grinning.

However, to her dismay, when the concert was over, not a single person (and certainly not Ms. Angelo) mentioned Broadway. All Ruby heard were comments about how much money had been raised and how the community center might be saved after all, blah, blah, blah. In the car on the way home, Min did say, "Ruby, you did a terrific job. I'm mighty proud of you." But again, no mention of Broadway.

Mr. Pennington had no sooner called good night to Min, Flora, and Ruby and was walking to his front door when Flora poked her sister and said, "Are you going to tell her now?"

Ruby climbed out of the car. "I have until Wednesday, you know." But even as she said the words she knew that Wednesday would be no better than tonight.

"So you're going to wait after all?" asked Flora.

"No," Ruby answered crossly. "I'm going to do it now."

And she did.

The moment they were inside and Min was locking the door behind them, Ruby said, "Min? Can I talk to you?"

"Sure, honey."

"We should probably go sit down."

Min glanced at her granddaughter. "This sounds serious."

"I guess it is."

Min sat on the couch in the living room, and Ruby sat opposite her in an armchair, King Comma in her lap for comfort. Ruby knew that Flora was lurking somewhere nearby but decided not to do anything about it.

"Well?" said Min when Ruby had sat mutely in front of her for nearly a minute. She offered Ruby a smile.

"It's sort of a long story," Ruby began.

"I hope it isn't too long. This is a school night," Min reminded her.

"Okay. Well, the thing is . . . one day I was looking through your drawers —"

"Excuse me?" said Min. "You were snooping in my drawers?"

Ruby rushed on, even though she thought she heard a snort from the direction of the dining room. "No, not snooping. Not technically. I was bored, so I was looking around, um, in your bedroom, and I found the box with Mom's things in it and I just wanted to see them. I saw that glass owl and I took it out and then I dropped it and it broke."

Min was frowning now. Ruby had intended to barge ahead with the story, but she stopped to apologize. "I'm really sorry. It was an *accident*. I didn't *mean* to break anything."

"Ruby —" Min started to say, a warning in her voice.

"And you won't believe all the good things that happened just because I broke the owl. But before I get to that part of the story, I have something to show you." Ruby didn't risk waiting for a response. She flew from the room, ran upstairs, and returned carrying the cardboard box from Min's desk. She pulled the rubber band off, lifted the lid, and placed the box on the couch next to her grandmother.

Min glanced in the box. Then she took a closer look. She lifted the owl out. "I thought you said you broke it."

Ruby realized that Flora was now standing in the

doorway between the living room and the dining room, and she flashed her sister a triumphant smile.

"I did. But I worked and worked and worked and saved all my money and bought you another owl. See? You didn't notice any difference."

Min was turning the owl over in her hands. "It *isn't* the same owl," she finally murmured.

"I wasn't going to tell you, but Flora said I had to."

Ruby wasn't sure what might happen next, but she didn't expect to see Min's eyes suddenly grow bright with tears. She stared, horrified, at her grandmother, whose chin quivered and whose finger shook as she ran it along the smooth glass.

"Where's the other owl?" Min asked.

"The other owl?" Something else Ruby hadn't expected. "It — it was in pieces so I threw it away. Actually, Flora vacuumed a chunk of it up —"

"*Before* I knew what had happened!" exclaimed Flora. She ran into the living room and flung herself down next to Min. "See, Ruby?" she said furiously. "I told you Min would be upset."

"Which is exactly why I didn't want to say anything."

"Ruby," said Min. "I think you need to tell me the whole story, from start to finish. Without any excuses. Just the story."

So Ruby told her about the past few months — about the Self-Improvement Plan and the rude man in the jewelry store and her fight with Flora. When she reached the part about the fight, Min said, "Ah. So that explains things."

"Anyway," said Ruby at last, "I'm very, very, very sorry, Min. *Very* sorry." She lowered her eyes and then raised them to meet her grandmother's. "Do you forgive me?"

"Yes, Ruby, of course I forgive you."

"Oh, thank you!"

"This isn't the end of the subject, though."

"It isn't? But it's getting late," said Ruby, pretending to yawn. (She had perfected fake yawning.)

"No. You need to understand something." Min handed the owl back to Ruby. "Thank you very much, but I don't want to keep this."

"You don't? But I worked so hard for it."

"That isn't the point. Ruby, what you did was wrong." (To her credit, Flora chose not to smirk at Ruby when Min uttered these words.) "You were snooping, you broke something of mine, and you didn't tell me about it. I understand that you tried to fix things, but you *knew* that what you had done was wrong. Otherwise, you wouldn't have tried to cover it up. And there's more. The owl — the original one — was very special to me. It wasn't that it was expensive. It wasn't even that it was your mother's. It was what the owl represented. It had been in our family for a long time. It was a gift to me from my parents when I left for college. The owl is a symbol of wisdom, after all. When your mother went away to college, I passed the owl down to her, since she was the older of my daughters. And your mother was going to give it to Flora when *she* went to college.

"Because of all this," Min continued, "the owl was one of the few things that belonged to your mother that I decided to keep." Min's voice wobbled, and Ruby stared down at King Comma. "I think of her every day, you know. There are reminders of her everywhere, especially in your face, Ruby, and in yours, Flora. But sometimes I simply need to go to my room and be alone and hold on to something of hers. That's why the box is in my desk."

For several moments, no one spoke. Ruby listened to King Comma's rumbly purr. Finally, she said, "I'm sorry," in a very small voice, and this time she actually meant it.

"I know you are," Min replied. "But there are going to be consequences, Ruby. I'll have to think what they'll be. We can discuss that subject tomorrow. For now, there's something else."

Ruby nodded, and despite the hour, Min then delivered a very long talk (to both her and Flora, Ruby couldn't help noticing) about privacy and trust. And *then* Min surprised Ruby once again. "I'm just wondering," she said, "if there might have been another reason you took the owl out of the box."

"What do you mean?"

"Maybe you *thought* you wanted to introduce the owl to your china animals, but what you really wanted was to have something else of your mother's. I know you have a few things — you, too, Flora — but maybe the owl made you think of your mother and you wanted to have another reminder of her."

It was Ruby's turn for a quivering chin, and she found that her throat felt so tight that she couldn't speak. She merely nodded her head as hot tears began to fall.

"Come here," said Min, and Ruby set King Comma aside and flopped onto the couch with her head in Min's lap. Flora leaned against Min's shoulder. "You know that you girls can always talk to me about your parents, don't you?" asked Min.

"Yes," whispered Flora.

Ruby nodded her head in Min's lap.

"It's been more than two years since they died," Min went on, "but that doesn't mean we miss them any less."

"I think about them every day," said Flora.

"Me, too," Ruby managed to say.

Min reached across Ruby for the shoe box. "Maybe this doesn't belong in my desk," she said finally. "Maybe it belongs down here where we can all look in it."

"Maybe we could put the things out where we can see them," suggested Flora.

"I don't like them hidden," added Ruby.

"Fair enough," said Min. She glanced at her watch. "And now I believe it's bedtime. Past bedtime. Ruby, we'll finish our talk tomorrow."

Exhausted, Ruby kissed Min good night and climbed the stairs to her room.

CHAPTER 16

Excuses

Margaret Malone sat at the desk in her bedroom and stared at the wall. On the wall was a bulletin board and pinned to it were photos and greeting cards and a button that said CHICKEN LITTLE WAS RIGHT and a string of plastic beads and the letter telling her that she'd been accepted at Smith College. But Margaret didn't see any of those things. Her mind was on the conversation she'd had with her sister that morning.

While she and Lydia and their father had grabbed breakfast — her father had eaten his toast standing over the sink, and Margaret had entered the kitchen just as Lydia was getting ready to leave the house — Margaret had said, "I'm almost ready for the party. I even found confetti that looks like graduation caps."

"Oh, I meant to tell you," Lydia had replied, "I can't come to the party."

"What? Why? I told you the date two weeks ago."

"I know, but I forgot it, and then I accepted a sitting job and I don't want to tell the people I can't come after all. I've never sat for them before. They'll think I'm unreliable if I back out now."

It had been on the tip of Margaret's tongue to say, "So you'd rather disappoint your sister by skipping her one and only high school graduation party?" Instead, she'd said nothing as Lydia had breezed out of the house.

"Do you want me to talk to her?" Dr. Malone had asked.

Margaret had shaken her head. Now, at the end of the day, she was sitting at her desk, staring into space. She was supposed to be studying for final exams. Everyone kept asking her why she cared about her senior finals since she'd already been accepted at one of the top colleges in the country. But Margaret cared a lot. She didn't want to spoil her record. She also knew that this was just one of the many things that set her apart from Lydia — who didn't even care about her sophomore year finals and probably also didn't care whether she got into any college whatsoever.

Margaret's father had offered to talk to Lydia about the party, but Margaret knew she had to do that herself. So the moment she heard the front door open and close she went downstairs.

"Hey," she said to her sister.

"Hey."

"Guess what. I found this party site where you can order decorations and stuff for any kind of party."

"Cool," said Lydia, who actually sounded vaguely interested.

"So I ordered plastic cups with diplomas on them, and napkins with my name and class year on them, and favors that — well, I don't want to spoil the surprise, since you'll get one, too. And I'm still within the budget Dad gave me."

"That's great, Margaret. Really."

"Lydia, won't you come? Please?"

"I told you I can't. This job is important. I'm hoping to sit for these people all summer. I need the money."

"But it's my graduation. And I'll be leaving for Smith in four months. Less than four months."

Lydia sighed. "Well, maybe I can do both. I'll come to the end of your party after I get home from sitting."

Margaret returned to her room. She was not going to let Lydia ruin the party. Her father had said she could plan a party for her friends, he had generously offered to pay for it, and Margaret planned to have a happy evening whether her sister was there or not.

The nice thing about working at Heaven, Margaret thought two days later as she rang up a customer and handed him his bag, was that it was so straightforward. She didn't have to think much about the time she spent there. She stocked the displays and stamped HEAVEN on the cardboard jewelry boxes and made change and that was about it. There were few decisions to be made, no feelings got hurt, and rarely was anyone disappointed by anything. She simply showed up, did as she was told, and left. And got paid for it. It was a pleasant, if dull, break from finals and sisters and major life decisions. Also, she enjoyed talking to the customers.

"Hi, Margaret!" called Flora one hot afternoon when, even though it was only May, people were already seeking air-conditioning. Flora closed the door quickly behind her and sagged against the checkout counter. "Min said it's supposed to be ninety degrees tomorrow. Actually, she said, 'Lawsy, it's going to be ninety tomorrow.'"

Margaret laughed. "Can I help you with anything?"

"I'm looking for a present for my friend Annika. You know, my old friend, the one who visited last summer?" Margaret nodded. "Except that I really don't know what to get her."

"What kind of jewelry does she wear?"

"I'm not sure."

"Does she have pierced ears?"

"She said she was going to get them pierced, but I don't know if she did."

"Are you sure you should be shopping for her in a jewelry store?"

Now Flora laughed. "No." Then she added, "Oh, we got the invitation to your party! Thank you. We're all coming."

"That's great!"

"I've never been to a graduation party before. Who else will be there?"

"Well, apart from my dad, let's see —"

"Lydia's coming, isn't she?"

Margaret shook her head. "She can't. She's going to be busy." Then she added, "You're lucky. You and Ruby are so close. Lydia and I used to be close, too, but after Mom died we sort of drifted apart. I thought the opposite would happen. I guess . . . I don't know. Anyway, like I said, you're lucky. You and Ruby are the closest sisters I've ever known. Even after everything that's happened to you. Or maybe because of it . . . Flora? Are you okay?"

Flora had stepped away from the counter. Margaret saw a bright pink blush creep across her face. "Yeah," Flora said and then paused. "You and Lydia really used to be close?"

"As close as you and Ruby."

"Wow."

"I always thought one day things would be the same again, that we'd just drift on back together. But that hasn't happened."

"Maybe it will," said Flora in a small voice. "It still might. You never know."

"Are you sure you're okay?"

"Yup. Just hot. So who else is coming to the party?"

"Almost everyone at the Row Houses and six of my friends."

"But not Lydia?"

"No. Well, she might come for a few minutes at the end. The truth is, she *could* come to the party, but I don't think she wants to."

Flora nodded. "I'd better go," she said. "See you later. Thank you again for the invitation."

Margaret watched Flora leave Heaven and wondered what was wrong.

CHAPTER 17

Surprise!

Olivia sat on her front stoop and watched the world of Aiken Avenue as it came to life on the first day of Memorial Day weekend. She called good morning to Mr. Pennington as he hurried down his front walk, being gently pulled along by an exuberant Variety. She waved to her neighbors across the way, who clearly planned to spend the day working in their flower beds. She watched the Fongs leave for Main Street, all of them apparently off to work together, Mr. Fong pushing Grace in her stroller, and Mrs. Fong walking their two corgis, who, catching sight of Variety, strained at their leashes and barked before touching noses with him.

Olivia yawned. She felt pleased and lazy and excited all at the same time. The day was bright and warm, but not nearly as hot as it had been. When Olivia had come downstairs that morning, her mother had announced, "Off goes the air-conditioning. We'll open all the windows!" Now, as Olivia sat outside, her parents' murmuring voices drifted to her through the living room window. Above her, two barn swallows chattered to each other in the maple tree. Olivia breathed deeply and caught the scents of pine and lavender and newly turned earth and sun-warmed flagstones. It was a perfect spring day.

On top of that, only two and a half more weeks of school were left, and the final few days would be devoted to assemblies and a field trip and cleaning out lockers. So really, Olivia thought, it's like nine days are left. Several of them would consist of tests and the presentation of projects, but Olivia chose not to think of those things at that particular moment. The long weekend stretched ahead of her and she planned to enjoy it. Maybe she would help out at Sincerely Yours later, but only if she felt like it. She knew she wouldn't actually be needed. And this brought to mind another happy thought: Her parents had recently told her that despite the difficult year, the store seemed to be holding its own. Very few changes had been made after all, and the summer's tourist business, which officially began that very day, would only improve things.

Olivia yawned and stretched and glanced up as Min opened her front door and leaned outside to bring in the newspaper. "Hi!" Olivia called, but her mood darkened slightly. The only bad things in her life at the moment were right next door: Flora and Ruby, who were still mad at each other.

"Or at least Flora is still mad at Ruby," Olivia had said to Nikki the previous day as they left school together.

"The fight was about an owl!" Nikki had exclaimed. "A glass owl. I don't get it."

"I don't think we know the whole story."

"We know that Ruby did something wrong —"

"According to Flora," Olivia had interrupted.

"Well, anyway, Flora said Ruby told Min what she'd done, so now everything is out in the open."

"But their fight doesn't seem to be over."

"Things are better, though, don't you think?" Nikki had asked tentatively. "They seem a little better."

"But not the same as before."

"No, not the same as before."

Now, replaying this conversation in her mind, Olivia jumped to her feet. With great determination she marched inside, found the phone, and brought it into her room. She dialed Nikki's number. "Okay," she said the moment she heard her friend's voice, "we have to do something about Flora and Ruby. And this time we *really* have to do something, not just talk about it."

"Good morning to you, too," replied Nikki.

Olivia laughed. "Sorry. Good morning. It's just that I was thinking about Flora and Ruby, and, I don't know, the long weekend is here, and school's almost over, and everything should be great. But it's like there's this wall between us, and Flora and Ruby. And we didn't put it there."

Nikki sighed. "I know what you mean."

"So I had an idea: Maybe it's time to carry out our plan."

"What plan?"

"The one we came up with when we were talking about going on a Saturday adventure."

"The plan we thought could blow up in our faces?"

"Well, yeah. Only now I don't think that will happen. Things are different. Flora and Ruby have started to work out their problem." Olivia paused. "Look. What's the worst that can happen?"

"What we said before: Flora and Ruby will wind up mad at us for interfering."

"But then they'd be mad at each other *and* mad at us. Do you really think that's what they want?"

"No."

"Besides, by now it feels like the fight has been going on forever. At this point I really don't think we have anything to lose."

"I'm not sure I agree with you," said Nikki cautiously. "But I don't think that *not* interfering has gotten us anywhere, either."

"Excellent! So let's go back to our original plan."

"Pizza?"

"Well, no, not pizza. But inviting them to something — and not telling Flora that Ruby is invited and vice versa. And we have to come up with something really special, something they'll both definitely want to do."

"The mall?" suggested Nikki.

"Nah. Too hard to talk there. And I think we'll need to talk."

"Not pizza?"

"It has to be better than that."

There was a long pause, and finally Nikki said, "I have an idea. What if we had a sleepover at my house tonight? We've never done that before, and . . . Ooh, I know. We could sleep outside! I'll have to ask my mom about this, but I'm sure she'll say it's okay."

"A campout in your yard? Wow, that *would* be fun," said Olivia slowly.

"It's different."

"Flora and Ruby would both really want to come."

"We'd have a chance to talk."

Finally, Olivia exclaimed, "It's brilliant!"

"Now we just have to make it work. How are we going to get Flora and Ruby — separately — to my house?"

"Let me think for a sec." Olivia frowned and turned her face toward the ceiling. "Okay. How about if you call Ruby and invite her — after you check with your mother, of course. Tell Ruby you're only inviting her. No one else. Then I'll call Flora and tell her we're having an end-of-seventh-grade sleepover, just the three of us. That way she won't be suspicious when I don't mention Ruby."

"That's good," said Nikki. "But how are Flora and

Ruby going to get here? Min can't drive them together or they'll figure out what's going on."

"Well, I'll tell Flora that my dad can drive both of us. I'm pretty sure he'll be able to."

"Great. And I'll ask Ruby if Min can bring her over. My mom won't be able to pick her up. She has to work today."

"Oh, you know what? We're going to have to tell Min what we're doing. She'll have to be in on the plan. That's okay, though. I have a feeling she'll like it."

"Now we just have to hope that Flora doesn't mention the sleepover to Ruby, and Ruby doesn't mention it to Flora."

"That won't happen. That's the only good thing about their fight."

By lunchtime, all the plans were in place. Nikki had phoned her mother at Three Oaks and gotten permission to host her very first sleepover, and a campout at that. Nervous and excited, she had called Olivia back with the news. "Mom said yes! Oh, this is going to be so much fun. You guys have never slept over before."

"I've never slept outside before," Olivia had said.

"Mom's going to stop by the store on the way home and get hot dogs and stuff. We can cook out, too. Should I call Ruby now?"

"Definitely."

So Nikki had invited Ruby to the sleepover, and fifteen minutes later, Olivia had invited Flora. Driving arrangements were made, and by five-thirty that afternoon, Olivia and Flora were on their way to the Shermans'. Twice Flora glanced at Olivia and said, "Are you all right? You look kind of funny."

"Just excited, I guess. I've never been to an outdoor sleepover."

Olivia then consulted her watch four times before her father pulled into the Shermans' driveway. If all went according to plan, Ruby and Min would arrive in half an hour.

Mr. Walter had barely applied the brakes when Olivia flung her door open and shot out of the car. Nikki flew across her yard. "You're here!" she cried breathlessly.

Flora watched her friends and frowned. "You guys, we just saw each other yesterday."

"I know, but this is going to be so much fun!" shrieked Olivia.

"Mom bought stuff for s'mores!" added Nikki at top volume. Then, catching the look on Flora's face, she added graciously, "Come on inside. Put your sleeping bags and things downstairs. We'll set everything up outside later."

The next half hour was spent trying to calm down both Mae and Paw-Paw, who seemed as excited as Nikki and Olivia.

"Can I sleep outside, too?" Mae wanted to know.

Mrs. Sherman was in the middle of explaining why she could not, when Paw-Paw let out one loud bark, and Mae left her mother, ran to the front door, and cried, "Someone else is here!"

Olivia reached for Nikki's hand and gripped it. She tightened her grasp when Mae said, "Hey, it's Ruby! I didn't know she was coming, too."

"Neither did I," said Flora, narrowing her eyes at Nikki and Olivia.

"You stay here," Nikki commanded Flora, and ran outside. A minute later, she returned with Ruby. Min's car was disappearing down the lane.

The sisters stood in the Shermans' kitchen and glared at each other.

"Now, before you say anything," said Olivia, "just listen to Nikki and me, okay?" No one said a word, so Olivia continued. "You . . ." (she gave her full attention to Flora and Ruby) "*have* to make up. Nikki and I have been talking about this, and we hate seeing you so mad at each other. We all used to be friends, and now it feels like we're coming apart. I miss what we used to be. Nikki does, too. So would you *please* make up?"

"Okay," said Flora instantly.

"What?" said Olivia and Nikki.

"Okay. I'm sorry. Ruby, I don't want to keep fighting. Do you?"

Ruby shook her head.

"Is the fight over, then?" asked Olivia.

"Yeah," said Ruby.

"Wow," said Nikki. "That was easy."

CHAPTER 18

By the Light of the Moon

"Would you guys please stop crying?" begged Nikki.

"Only Flora and Ruby are crying," pointed out Mae, who was sitting at the kitchen table, openly staring at the older girls. "Is this what you do at sleepovers?"

"Not usually," Nikki replied. She ran to the bathroom, found a box of tissues, returned to the kitchen, and set it on the table. "Um, Mae, could you go help Mom for a few minutes?"

"Help her with what?"

"I don't know. Whatever she needs help with."

"But this is more interesting."

"Mae!"

"*Okay, okay.*"

Mae stomped upstairs, keeping her eyes on the kitchen until the last possible moment.

"I'm sorry I was mad for so long!" Flora said, pulling three tissues from the box and wadding them up in her fist.

"I'm sorry about snooping," replied Ruby, wiping her eyes. "And for calling you a judgmental hag."

"You called her that?" said Olivia.

"In my head I did."

"Now that everything is over," said Nikki, "could you tell us what happened?"

"It *is* over, isn't it?" asked Olivia in a small voice.

"It's over." Flora glanced at her sister. "Is it okay to tell them?"

Ruby nodded. "I guess so. You can tell them everything except . . ." She thought for a moment and then leaned over and whispered in Flora's ear.

"All right," agreed Flora. And she told Olivia and Nikki all that had happened up until the moment Min had handed the replacement owl back to Ruby and told her she didn't want to keep it. Everything from that point on was private, not to be shared even with their best friends.

"Boy," said Nikki when Flora finally finished speaking. "I don't know what to say."

"Then let's not talk about it anymore," replied Flora. "We're here to have fun."

"All four of us," said Olivia.

"All four of us," agreed Flora. "Together."

"Girls?" called Mrs. Sherman from upstairs. "Is it okay if we come down now?"

"Yes!" chorused Flora, Ruby, Nikki, and Olivia.

"Good, because if we're going to have hot dogs and s'mores, then I should start the grill." Mrs. Sherman headed down the stairs, followed by Mae, who was dragging a sleeping bag behind her.

"Mom!" wailed Nikki, and Mrs. Sherman turned around, saw the sleeping bag, and shook her head.

"Toads!" Mae exclaimed, and threw the sleeping bag back upstairs. "Fudgesicles!"

"But you can eat supper with us, Mae," said Nikki generously. "You, too, Mom."

The sun hadn't set yet, but it was edging toward the horizon by the time the outdoor feast was ready.

"Spread this on the ground, honey," Mrs. Sherman said to Mae, handing her an ancient tablecloth.

"Oh, a real picnic!" said Mae joyfully. "Eating right on the ground, just like in a movie."

Flora and Ruby and their friends carried dish after dish outside — corn on the cob, potato salad, pickles, cornbread, slices of watermelon. Mrs. Sherman disappeared into the house and returned with a pitcher of iced tea and another of lemonade.

"This is the perfect picnic," said Flora. "Thank you so much."

"I'm happy we can do this," said Nikki shyly.

And Flora knew exactly what her friend meant, since two years earlier nothing like this could have taken place at the Shermans' house.

"Ah," said Ruby as she sank onto a corner of the tablecloth and surveyed the food.

The air was growing cooler. Flora heard first one

peeper and then another. A mourning dove twittered as it whooshed into the air.

"We saw an owl last night," remarked Mae as her mother handed around plates, and Ruby dipped her head.

Flora helped herself to a hot dog and a slice of watermelon. "I can't believe summer is here."

"Technically it isn't here until school is out," said Ruby.

"Well, *technically* it isn't here until June twenty-second," commented Olivia. "But who cares?"

Flora ate and laughed and talked and filled her plate again and eventually declared, "I'm stuffed!"

"Save room for s'mores," said Mrs. Sherman.

They waited until darkness had fallen and then stood around the grill, toasting marshmallows in the glowing coals.

"This is the messiest sandwich I ever ate," commented Mae, wiping chocolate from her face with fingers that were coated with marshmallow and crumbs. "Oh, well. It's a good thing I'm going to be sleeping outside tonight. It won't matter if I'm messy."

"Mom!" cried Nikki.

"Mae," said her mother.

"Toads!"

The night was blacker than Flora had imagined it would be. By the time Mrs. Sherman had doused the flames in the grill and taken Mae inside to bed, and

Flora and her friends had arranged their sleeping bags in a tight circle in the grass beneath an oak tree, it was after ten o'clock. And very, very dark.

"Isn't there supposed to be moonlight or something?" asked Ruby.

"What would the 'or something' be?" Olivia wanted to know.

"Big, giant streetlights?" ventured Ruby.

"Out *here*?" said Nikki.

Flora wriggled farther down in her sleeping bag. "If an animal came along," she said, "would we be able to see it?"

Next to her, Ruby shot out of her own sleeping bag and rose to her feet. "What kind of animal?"

"Does it matter?" asked Nikki, giggling.

"I don't think this is funny," said Ruby, but she sat down.

"It's a little funny," said Olivia.

"What kind of wild animals do you have out here, Nikki?" asked Ruby.

"Oh, you know. Bears and pumas. Rattlesnakes. Things like that."

Ruby was on her feet again in an instant. "What, are you kidding me?"

"Yes," said Nikki. "Well, actually, I have seen bears a couple of times, but I really don't think we have to worry."

Ruby moaned. "I hope we make it through the night," she muttered.

"Well, I'm having a good time," said Nikki.

"Me, too," agreed Olivia. "But, um, Nikki? I have to use the bathroom."

"Okay. I'll go in with you."

Flora was tempted to say, "And leave Ruby and me out here all defenseless?" But she simply slid her sleeping bag nearer to her sister's and listened as her friends' footsteps trailed off in the darkness. "Ruby?" she whispered.

"Yeah."

"I'm right here if you need me."

"I know."

"I really am sorry about our fight."

"I know that, too. And I really am sorry about all the things I did."

"You know what Margaret Malone told me the other day?"

"No."

"She said that she and Lydia used to be close — as close as you and me — but that they've grown apart. And they just keep growing further and further apart."

"That's sad."

"Yeah. And I don't want it to happen to us."

"It won't. Why would you think that?"

"Why would I *think* that?! Because of our fight. And because, I don't know, you and I aren't the same people who moved here two years ago. Remember when we first came to Camden Falls, how we spent all our time together? Well, most of it, anyway. And I felt like you needed me to take care of you."

Ruby sat up. "I did need you to take care of me."

"Don't you need me now?"

"Of course! You're my sister. But we're older, and lots of things have changed. We go to different schools, and I'm friends with Lacey and Hilary, and I have my classes and the Children's Chorus, and you have . . . you have, um . . ."

"Sewing and baby-sitting and volunteering at Three Oaks."

"Right."

"Actually," said Flora slowly, "I guess we wouldn't want things to be exactly the way they were when we first moved here. We were so sad then. And we hardly knew anyone."

"We kind of clung to each other," said Ruby.

"Now we're part of the Row Houses and part of Main Street."

"But we do still have each other. We always will, you know."

"Even if our lives go off in different directions," said Flora. "I just really, really don't want to end up like Margaret and Lydia."

"We won't." Ruby paused. "Uh-oh. Now *I* have to go to the bathroom. And I am not walking through the dark alone."

Flora reached for her sister's hand. "You don't have to. I'll come with you."

Twenty minutes later Flora, Ruby, Nikki, and Olivia were settled in their sleeping bags again. They tried very hard to fall asleep. After fifteen minutes they gave up. They talked, they sang, and finally they told ghost stories, which turned out to be a bad idea.

"So then," said Flora, coming to the end of an eerie story that Annika had once told her, "the old woman said to the traveling stranger, 'But you couldn't have spoken with my daughter out there on that lonesome, deserted highway. My daughter died ten years ago.'"

"*Aughhh!*" shrieked Olivia. "You just gave me the shivers!"

"Me, too," said Nikki in a whisper, and Flora noted that Nikki had covered her head with a T-shirt.

"Hey, you guys," said Ruby, peering at the glowing dial of her watch. "Guess what."

"What?" said Olivia.

"It's midnight."

"Ooh," moaned Flora, Olivia, and Nikki.

There was silence for a few moments, and then Ruby said, "What was that?"

"What was what?" asked Olivia in a voice so tiny that Flora could barely hear her.

"That sound," whispered Ruby. "I thought I heard footsteps."

"I didn't hear anything," said Nikki.

"*Shh!* Just listen." Ruby sat up. "Hear that? It's a sort of crunching sound. Like feet walking through dead leaves."

"Okay, that's it!" Flora slithered out of her sleeping bag and got to her feet. Immediately, she felt a hand on her shoulder. "*Aughhh!* Someone's got me!"

"It's *me!*" cried Olivia.

"I can't take this anymore!" yelped Ruby.

Nikki gathered her sleeping bag under her arm in an untidy bundle. "Everybody inside!"

In an instant, Flora, Nikki, Olivia, and Ruby were running across the Shermans' yard. Nikki yanked open her front door. She dropped her sleeping bag on the living room floor. "We can finish our sleepover here," she said.

"Yeah, here is good," agreed Olivia.

"Maybe I'll just leave this light on," added Nikki.

"Is the door locked?" asked Flora.

"Yes, but we should probably shove that table in front of it."

At last, Flora and Ruby and their friends were settled on the floor, lights blazing, unable to fall asleep.

"We should do this again," said Ruby.

CHAPTER 19

Needle and Thread

Coffee cup in hand, Min Read stood at the counter in Needle and Thread and admired the two quilts that were hanging, one on each side of the store. There was Lacey Morris's square on which she had painted Camden Falls Elementary School. There was Mary Woolsey's square, the flowers in her own gardens blooming in brilliantly colored ribbons. There was Gigi's square showing the front of Needle and Thread. And there were squares depicting the Row Houses, the mayor, Main Street, and people and events in Camden Falls history.

"Amazing," murmured Min out loud. She walked to the front of the store and stood at the door, sipping her coffee and watching Main Street come to life on a bright June morning. She cherished these few moments alone, when town was quiet and she could gather her thoughts.

The quilts, she decided, were, if not quite master-pieces, then surely fabulous enough to bring in quite a bit of money for the community center. She and Gigi and Flora had spent hours stitching and piecing until every last square had been fitted into just the right spot. A true community effort.

And this Saturday was the big day. In less than an hour, Needle and Thread would open its door (liter-ally, thought Min, since the weather was fine and the door to the store could stand open all day long), and by noon an auctioneer would arrive and the festivities would begin.

Min closed her eyes briefly. When she opened them, she saw before her the Main Street of her childhood — the Woolworth's, where she could buy a hair ribbon for a penny, and Jugtown, where she could buy candy for a penny. She could buy lots of things for a penny in those days. Nowadays, people didn't think much of pennies. Last week a customer had dropped the change that Min had handed her. When a penny had rolled under the counter, she'd waved her hand and said, "Oh, never mind. It's just a penny." Thinking of penny candy and penny hair ribbons, Min hadn't replied.

Min blinked her eyes again, and now she saw Main Street as it had looked when she was a young mother raising two daughters. There was Piccadilly, the cloth-ing store where she had bought tiny knee socks and nighties and the red sandals the girls wore in the summer. There was Buxton's, the restaurant that had eventually become the T-shirt Emporium.

Min blinked, and there were her daughters all grown up and working together at Dutch Haus one summer. Blink, and her daughters had moved away. Blink, and Frannie was visiting Camden Falls with her own daughters. Min remembered watching Flora explore Needle and Thread when she was four years old and asking for a piece of fabric so she could make a dress for her cat. Which cat was that? Min wondered now. The one that was named Pampered Princess, as if it were a racehorse? On that visit, Min recalled, she had had a long talk with Frannie, telling her that she planned to retire in ten years.

"But why?" her daughter had asked. "I thought you loved the store."

"I do. But I'm getting older. I wouldn't mind if my days slowed down a bit. Do you know how many books I haven't read?"

"Well, probably thousands," Frannie had replied. "Millions."

"I mean, how many classics. I haven't read *The Mayor of Casterbridge* or *The Brothers Karamazov* or *Penrod*. I haven't even read *Wuthering Heights*."

"Well —" Frannie had started to say.

"And I want time for sewing. I mean, my own sewing. It's been years since I made a blouse for myself just because I wanted one, not because we needed to display it in the window. And there are boxes in the attic that I need to sort through, and drawers that need to be cleaned out. When I die, I don't want you —"

"Mother!" Frannie had exclaimed. "No one is going to die. Stop talking like that."

"All right. But I'd still like to retire. I can afford to."

Blink, and six years had gone by, and Frannie had died, her husband, too, and Flora and Ruby were living with Min, and Min could no longer afford to retire after all.

"Hi, Min! We're here!"

Min smiled and set her coffee cup on the table at the front of the store. "Hi, girls."

Flora, Ruby, and Olivia ran through the door of Needle and Thread, giggling and shouting. Sometimes, thought Min, the very sight of them eased the pain in her aching joints, and she instantly turned her thoughts to dance recitals and homework and summer vacation.

"Is everything ready?" asked Flora at the same time that Olivia exclaimed, "Oh, there are the quilts. They look great!"

"Every last thing is ready," replied Min. "Olivia, your grandmother will be here in a few minutes. You girls can help us set out the food. People should start arriving around eleven-thirty, and the auction will take place at noon."

"Is the auctioneer coming?" asked Ruby.

Min nodded. A professional auctioneer had volunteered to help out at the event.

"That would be a cool job," said Ruby. "I'd like to be an auctioneer. 'Bid now! Bid now! Fifty! Fifty! Do I hear fifty? Fifty from the bald man in front! Now how about sixty! Sixty! How about seventy-five? SOLD to the rich lady who won't stop waving her hand around.' Except you have to talk so fast that people can hardly understand you."

"Well, I don't think our auctioneer will speak quite that fast," said Min. "But I do hope he'll help us get a good price for the quilts."

"And for the community center," said Olivia.

"Exactly."

Everyone was helping out. Up and down Main Street, sidewalk sales were being set up and a portion of the day's proceeds from almost every store and restaurant in town would be donated to the community center.

"There's the balloon guy!" called Ruby, looking out the window. "Oh, and I see the ice cream truck!"

At eleven-thirty, just a few minutes after Min and Gigi had temporarily closed the register and placed a sign in the window that said AUCTION STARTS AT NOON, Aunt Allie and Mr. Barnes wheeled Janie through the door. They were immediately followed by Mary Woolsey and then by Mr. Pennington, who was walking Variety.

"Hi, girls," said Mr. Barnes.

"Hi," replied Flora and Olivia, blushing furiously.

"Help yourselves to refreshments," added Gigi.

Min watched as the store filled up with friends and neighbors and customers and quite a few people she had never seen before. Robby Edwards marched in with his parents and a girl wearing a striped sundress.

"This is Sarah. She's my girlfriend," Robby announced proudly. "Would you like a cupcake, Sarah?"

Just before noon, Nikki arrived with her mother and Mae and Tobias. She waved to Min and Gigi and then joined Olivia, Ruby, and Flora, who were sitting on a couch at the front of the store, passing Janie from lap to lap.

Presently, Min checked her watch. "It's noon," she said to Gigi. "Do you want to do the honors?"

Gigi rang a bell, then cupped her hands around her mouth and called, "Hello, hello!" until the store grew quiet. "Thank you all for coming," she said. "I hope you're enjoying the refreshments. They were provided free of charge by Sincerely Yours, Dutch Haus, and College Pizza. I hope you've also had a chance to view the quilts you helped create," she continued. "Each square represents some aspect of our town or its history. The quilts are examples of your handiwork, and because they were a community effort they're also an example of what we can accomplish when we work together. So now, without further ado — I've always wanted to say that — I will turn you over to Billy Wonder, our auctioneer."

Billy Wonder. Min, who was now sitting on the couch, taking her turn at holding Janie, turned the name over in her head. That can't possibly be his real name, she decided. She clasped Janie's hands in her own and watched, fascinated, as the auction began.

"Let's start with three hundred dollars," said Billy, gesturing at one of the quilts.

Three hundred! Min would never have had the nerve to start with a figure so high. Which was exactly why, she soon realized, she would not make a good auctioneer. Almost immediately, Mr. Pennington's hand rose tentatively, and Billy Wonder cried, "Three hundred! Thank you, sir. Do I hear four hundred? Remember, this is for the community center."

At this point, Min closed her eyes. She felt terrible for Mr. Pennington, who had instantly been outbid, and at the same time both fascinated and grateful as she heard Billy Wonder ask for — and receive — bids of five hundred, then six hundred, then seven hundred fifty, and finally one thousand dollars.

"Min!" said Flora in an excited whisper, squeezing her grandmother's arm as the bidding continued. "You have to open your eyes. This is amazing!"

But Min couldn't look.

Not until Billy Wonder had sold the first quilt for three thousand seven hundred and fifty dollars and finally exclaimed, "Sold! The second quilt is yours, ma'am, for a cool five thousand dollars!" did Min manage to open her eyes again.

"Who bought them?" she asked Flora.

"I don't know the guy who bought the first one, but Mrs. DuVane bought the second one."

When the long day was at last over, when the sun was setting and pale shadows fell across Main Street and the air grew cooler and shopkeepers moved their wares back inside their stores and hosed down the sidewalks, Min and Gigi, alone in Needle and Thread, smiled tiredly at each other.

"What a day," said Gigi.

"The quilts raised almost nine thousand dollars," remarked Min. "It never occurred to me that they could pull in *that* much money. When the rest of the stores add their donations . . ."

"It was a good day for the community center," agreed Gigi. "And imagine, Sheila DuVane giving her quilt to the center so that it can be displayed there."

Min sighed. "She may be one of our more ornery customers, but she does have a good heart." She smiled again at her friend.

"Can I give you a lift home?" asked Gigi a few minutes later.

"Thank you, but I think I'll walk. It will give me a chance to clear my head."

Gigi left, and Min stood once more at the door and looked out at Main Street. She waved to Mrs. Grindle, who was closing up Stuff 'n' Nonsense. She caught sight of a balloon trapped high in the branches of a maple tree. She turned and looked behind her at the neat aisles of fabrics. Then she switched off the light, locked the door, and walked home to the Row Houses.

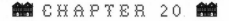

CHAPTER 20

The Row Houses

School was over. Report cards had been sent out. The long days of vacation had arrived. With July came Flora's first summer jobs. She was working three afternoons a week at Three Oaks. On the in-between afternoons, she was baby-sitting for Janie.

But her mornings were free, and so were her weekends, and on this Saturday her mind was busy with the event that would take place that evening: a Row House party.

"And we can hold it outdoors after all," she said to Ruby over breakfast. "The weather guy said it was going to rain today, but look outside. It's beautiful."

"What does the weather guy know?" remarked Ruby cheerfully. "So what are we supposed to do today to help get ready for the party?"

"Min wants us to organize something for the kids to do."

"How about a costume contest?"

"People need time to get ready for that," said Flora.

"A pet show?"

"I think Min meant something simpler."

"We could put on a skit."

"Well, maybe . . ."

"Yes! We could!" exclaimed Ruby, warming to the thought. "We have all day to rehearse. We could sing songs and then I could tap-dance. Then we could put on the skit, and then I could dance again. After that —"

"I don't know about the dancing," said Flora, "but the skit is a good idea. And maybe the songs."

"What's wrong with the dancing?"

Flora eyed her sister.

"I know. I know. It isn't all about me."

Flora smiled. "Come on. Let's go see who wants to be in the skit."

By late afternoon, the Row Houses were bustling. In the yard of every house, tables and chairs were being set out.

"Our yard is going to be, like, the playground," Alyssa Morris announced. "We got a waterslide yesterday, so wear your bathing suits over here."

"Which yard will have the desserts?" asked Ruby.

"Mine," Olivia replied. "Mom and Dad have been baking nonstop."

The party was to begin at six. At five-thirty, Flora stood on her back stoop. The promised rainy weather had continued to hold off. Flora looked to her left and saw, at the very end of the row, the waterslide in the Morrises' yard, as well as a softball and two bats, a stack of hula hoops, and several badminton rackets.

Next door, the Hamiltons' yard was quiet, but a folding table had been set out and covered with a blue checked cloth. The Hamiltons' first Row House party, thought Flora. She hadn't seen much of Mrs. Hamilton since she'd returned, and Willow had been pale and quiet lately, but the table was a good sign, and so was the fact that Cole had agreed to play a dog in the evening's skit. (Willow had said that she preferred to be a member of the audience.)

Flora sat on the stoop, and a few moments later she heard the door open behind her. "Hi, Min," she said without turning around.

"Hi, honey." Min groaned. "Oh, these old bones." But she managed to lower herself onto the stoop next to her granddaughter. "What are you thinking about?"

"The party, I guess. Well, really, I'm just thinking."

"I've always thought that this is the perfect time for thinking. The day is winding down, birds are returning to their nests. It's settling-in time."

"Not tonight it isn't!" exclaimed Ruby, and she hustled through the door and joined Flora and Min. "Tonight it's time to par-tay."

Min smiled. "What were you thinking about, Flora, or is it private?"

"My thoughts were sort of everywhere," Flora admitted. "I was thinking about tonight, but I was also thinking about the first Row House party we went to. Remember, Ruby?"

"Yup. People gave us presents."

"Ruby. Is that all you remember?"

"No. It was fun. It was the very first time we were all together. I mean, every single person in the Row Houses."

"It was only two years ago, but things were pretty different then," said Flora. "The Willets still lived here, and Mrs. Willet came to the party, even though she was confused."

"Mr. Pennington still had Jacques," said Ruby.

"Grace Fong hadn't been born."

"Robby didn't have a girlfriend." Ruby turned to Min. "Is it always like this?"

"Always like what?"

"Do things change all the time at the Row Houses?"

"Things change all the time everywhere."

"I know . . ."

"Did you have Row House parties when our mom and Aunt Allie were little?" asked Flora.

"We certainly did. And they weren't very different from the ones we have now. Except for the cast of characters."

Ruby smiled. "I like that. The cast of characters. Like we're a play and the Row Houses are the set.

Except that every time one of the characters changes, the play changes, too. In a real production, if someone left the play a new person would come in and take over his role and the same show would go on and on and on. But not in life. In life a new character changes everything."

"We're new characters," commented Flora. "You and I. We changed things when we moved here."

"You certainly did," said Min. She put her arms around her granddaughters.

"I'm really sorry about the owl," said Ruby suddenly.

"Now, where did that come from?" asked Min.

Ruby shrugged. "From things changing, I guess. And talking about Mom. Min? Do you think it's okay if I miss Mom and Dad every single day of my whole life? Even when I'm old?"

"Heavens! I know I'll miss them every single day of my life and I'm already as old as the hills."

"Can you believe I'll be in eighth grade this year?" asked Flora.

"And now where did *that* come from?" was Min's reply.

"More things changing. I'll be in eighth and Ruby will be in sixth. When we moved here, *I* was going into sixth grade."

"My land, such a lot of ruminating," said Min.

"Hey, Ruby!" yelled a voice from the direction of the Morrises' yard. "Go get your bathing suit!"

Ruby jumped to her feet and peered down the row of houses. She saw Lacey standing by her picnic table, clad in a rather skimpy bikini. "Okay!" she called back. She headed indoors. "Come on, you guys," she said to Min and Flora. "It's party time."

Later, when Flora looked back on the evening of the party, she liked to take one particular moment and relish it for its very ordinariness. She chose the moment just before the skit was to begin. By that time, a number of things, both ordinary and wonderful, had already taken place.

The evening had started punctually at six o'clock. That was when neighbors began to carry their supper contributions outside. A casserole was set down on the Hamiltons' table. Robby's father placed the first piece of chicken on the grill in the Edwardses' yard. Mr. Morris carried an enormous fruit salad past the waterslide and was nearly knocked over when Ruby tumbled to a stop at his feet. Mrs. Fong edged through her back door with a pitcher of iced tea. Olivia, concentrating furiously, set a pan of peach cobbler on the Walters' picnic table. Flora watched as the tables filled with lasagna, grilled vegetables, lemonade, ice cream, watermelon, hamburgers, chocolates, sodas. Someone even provided a plate of biscuits for the five resident dogs.

For more than an hour, every resident of the Row Houses wandered from yard to yard, chatting and laughing and eating. The children tried out the

Morrises' waterslide and, to Olivia's horror, so did her father. Flora played badminton with Margaret Malone. Lydia sat on her stoop and sent text messages to someone. Robby approached nearly everyone at the party and said, "Did you know I have a girlfriend?"

Just before eight o'clock, Olivia said to Flora, "We'd better put the skit on now before it gets too dark."

So Flora gathered the audience in her backyard, where they sat on lawn chairs waiting for the show, while Ruby gathered the kids in the kitchen, which had been designated backstage. And this was the ordinary moment that Flora chose to sear into her memory. Once again she stood on her stoop, and this time she looked at the faces of the expectant audience.

There were Willow and her parents sitting in a row, Mr. Hamilton in the middle, Willow edging her chair to one side to create as much distance from her parents as possible. Mr. Hamilton waited solemnly for the show to start. Mrs. Hamilton grinned broadly and gestured widely, but Flora didn't think she was talking to anyone.

There were Mr. and Mrs. Morris, holding hands and smiling fondly at Alyssa, who ran to them, exclaiming, "Ruby says I have natural talent!" before returning to the kitchen.

There was Mr. Pennington holding Variety in his lap and speaking softly to Min. He stroked Variety's ears, and Variety's feet twitched as he dreamed.

There were the Fongs, Grace perched in her father's lap, swinging her legs back and forth, Mrs. Fong smiling to herself. Earlier, she had shyly told the Row House neighbors that she and her husband were expecting another baby in November.

There were Olivia's parents murmuring to Min and Mr. Pennington.

There were Dr. Malone and Margaret, smiling at something Mrs. Edwards had just said. A little distance away from them, the only member of the audience seated on the ground, was Lydia, still sending texts and still looking as though she would rather be just about anywhere else.

There were the three Edwardses, waiting patiently. Robby had been invited to take part in the skit but had declined, politely saying that he was tired, but Flora knew the truth: He felt too old for such things. She supposed that one day she would feel too old, too. She hoped that day wouldn't come anytime soon. A part of her wanted to remain a Row House kid forever.

She turned and glanced at the nine cast members wiggling nervously in the kitchen and signaled to Ruby. It was time to start the show.

▓ CHAPTER 21 ▓

Camden Falls, Massachusetts

Have you ever been to Camden Falls, Massachusetts? If not, and if you're planning a trip there, you're in for a treat of the most ordinary kind — like vanilla ice cream when you have a choice of Moose Tracks and Rocky Road and Tropical Sunset. You chose vanilla because it's exactly what you want, and when it's exactly what you want, it doesn't seem ordinary at all.

Start your tour by standing on the corner of Dodds Lane and Main Street. Look south along Main. This is Camden Falls at the end of a hot day during a summer in which everyone hopes the tourist season will bring lots of visitors to town. And so far it's done just that. Walk along the street to the sixth store on the right. There is Needle and Thread, and at the open doorway is Min Read, one of the owners of the sewing shop. Min is gazing thoughtfully at a scene that she finds familiar and unfamiliar, constant and varying at the same time. She recalls a conversation she had with her granddaughter four months earlier. Min had remarked that Main Street looked shabby. Now she notes that lopsided signs have been rehung and fallen bricks have been replaced along with broken panes of glass. Buckets of paint have been hauled out of basements and put to good use, and with summer came flowers. Pots of them are hanging everywhere, boxes of flowers are blooming under the windows of the apartments that face Main Street, and the children of the community center's day-care program have planted a garden in the town square.

Even better, thinks Min, only one more store has closed, and in its place another has already opened. Surprisingly, Maty's Magic Store, which opened in the fall, is doing well. Who would have thought a magic store could survive in this economy? thinks Min.

Now walk back to the Marquis Diner. Dinner hour is about to begin and even on a weekday, the diner is bustling. Hilary Nelson, whose parents own the diner, is walking from table to table with a pitcher of water, filling glasses. It isn't the most interesting work she can think of, but she's grateful that the diner will remain open after a difficult start, and she doesn't care what it takes to keep it that way.

Turn around, cross the street, and walk along the other side of Main. There's Stuff 'n' Nonsense. Its owner, Gina Grindle, has been thinking about closing her store, but summer has brought enough customers so that now she's considering hiring part-time help.

There's Frank's Beans, the coffee shop, and there are Robby Edwards and Sarah. They're sitting at a table on the sidewalk, just the two of them. Their mothers are inside sipping coffee, but Robby and Sarah are in a world of their own. Robby reaches for Sarah's hand and says, "Do you want to go to the movies with me on Saturday?"

Now walk by the used bookstore, Dr. Malone's office, the post office, and the pet supply store. Turn left on Boiceville Road and ahead of you is the community center. It's open five days a week this summer instead of six, and basketball camp has been cancelled along with dance camp. Still, the director of the center is looking forward to a busy fall. At this very minute, Ruby Northrop and the members of the Children's Chorus are filing to the risers in the main hall, about to rehearse for another fund-raiser, which will take place the following week. Ruby is to sing a duet with Lacey Morris.

Now, if you need some exercise, come along for a hike into the countryside. Several miles away, set back from the county road, is a small house that was once far shabbier than Main Street ever looked. It, too, has had a coat of paint recently, though, missing pieces have been replaced, and crooked things have been set straight. The house belongs to Nikki Sherman and her family, and on this late afternoon, Nikki is in charge of starting supper. She wants it to be ready when her mother returns from work and her brother returns from his summer job at College Pizza. As she removes a head of lettuce from the refrigerator, her little sister, Mae, says to her, "Once upon a time a girl had a father. Then he disappeared." She looks at Nikki. "Do you like my fairy tale?"

"Is that the whole story?" Nikki asks.

"No. It ends with 'And she lived happily ever after.' But a lot of other things happen first."

Find your walking stick and return to Camden Falls. In a neighborhood not far from where Min Read lives with her granddaughters is a small house on a street with other small houses and plenty of children and babies and bicycles and dogs and wading pools. Walking across the street toward this house is a man who has just left his own home. He knocks on his neighbor's door and lets himself inside before the knock is answered. "Ready to go?" he calls. And a few minutes later, the man and a woman and a baby are strolling along the streets, calling hello to their neighbors. The man and the woman hold hands and smile at each other, and the baby calls out the second word she has learned: "Da-da!"

It's time to return to Main Street now. You will finish your tour at Needle and Thread, where earlier you met Min Read. The air is growing cooler as the light begins to fade. Stores are starting to close and shopkeepers call good night as they lower grates and turn keys and head for home, satisfied with the day. The door to Needle and Thread stands wide open. Inside, two young girls have flopped on the couches by the window. They are Flora and Ruby, Min's granddaughters. The rehearsal at the community center is over and Ruby is saying dramatically to her sister, "I'm exhausted! Simply exhausted!"

Flora grins. "Are you too tired for a sleepover?"

"What?"

"Min said we could have a sleepover tonight. I just called Nikki. Tobias is going to drive her over here."

At that moment, a wiry girl runs into the store and throws herself onto the couch next to Flora. This is Olivia. She and Flora and Ruby wait while their grandmothers close up the shop.

"There's Nikki!" Olivia cries suddenly.

Nikki climbs out of Tobias's car and runs to Needle and Thread. Flora and Olivia and Ruby are waiting for her. The girls link arms and walk down Main Street as a new moon rises over Camden Falls.

More ![MainStreet]
adventures are right around the corner!

#8: Special Delivery

Flora and Ruby are about to get their first cousin!

#9: Coming Apart

When Nikki's family hits a rough patch, her friends help her pull through.

#10: Staying Together

After a big fight, can sisters Ruby and Flora come together?

DON'T MISS A MEETING OF THE BSC!

READ THEM ALL!